Banner of Courage
By
Adrienne Hartman

Table of Contents

Preface

Abraham, Sarah, Isaac, Moses, David and Goliath are Jewish characters in the Old Testament composing part of God's plan for His chosen people of the Promised Land. The resurrection of Christ and the Holy Spirit in the New Testament are important elements of God's plan for the world at large.

"Banner of Courage" is a novel about God's plan for the future of Christianity. The author, Adrienne Hartman, writing from an evangelical perspective focuses on the centerpiece of the book Theodora Jackson, the daughter of a Black minister. Hartman's book describes the conflict between Theodora, her Native American Christian allies with the oppressive New World Order (NWO). Under the authority of NWO, the world becomes divided into ten regions, waving a flag of red and white with three black sixes fixed in a circle, and shutting down Christian churches, Christian schools, and home schooling.

Under these circumstances, like the characters and elements in the Bible, Theodora evolves into a key part of God's plan to save Christianity from the New World Order. By writing the book "Banner of Courage", Hartman foreshadows a future New World Order with its goal of destroying Christianity and the world in the need of a Savior.

Kermit L. Staggers, professor of political science
University of Sioux Falls

Introduction

Banner of Courage depicts a clash between good and evil, between God and Satan. A nation that was formed under God has become a cesspool of wickedness, one in which evil is regarded as good and good as evil. Christians have become criminals in the eyes of the New World Order (NWO) while rape and pillage is declared a good and acceptable way of life for those who work for the NWO.

Theodora, the heroine in the novel, is the central figure from the time she was born until the story ends. God has a special purpose for her and those who are close to her know this but nobody knows exactly what this plan is and it isn't fully revealed until the final chapter of the book.

The reader will be kept guessing what will happen next as Theodora's life takes on many twists and turns. Often she is faced with certain death only to be miraculously spared at the last moment.

It will seem like America has hopelessly fallen into a state from which even God can't rescue it. It may be disturbing to those who see a parallel today with the direction the country is moving in. But, take heart, there is a happy ending and God shows His hand and His power throughout the book.

The reader will discover that this is a God and country book. And those who put their trust in God will see One who constantly intervenes in the lives of those who love Him.

Chapter One

The House Church

It was a hot July Sunday morning in Topeka, KS and people were sneaking off to church all over the town. Services now were held in private homes ever since the NWO (New World Order Government) had outlawed all the places of worship and closed them down. They now served as museums or schools of indoctrination into the NWO belief system.

One of these little flocks of people huddled together inside the home of Reverend Hobart Jackson. It was the Westside Baptist Church and their little building had long since been confiscated. True believers weren't allowed to worship freely or openly any more. People's freedoms had been taken away one by one, ever since the last elected President had given up the country's sovereignty to the UN. Several years later it had morphed into the government system which was now called the NWO. This was under the control of a few elite men and women who manipulated the wealthy and used their money to operate this world dictatorship.

Reverend Jackson was a robust man who stood 6' 4" inches tall, a twelfth generation descendent of a slave in Georgia. Since his freedom from slavery, George Jackson had traveled to Kansas where he set up a lumber business. The township of Topeka eventually grew to be a town and eventually a city. Because of all the people who were moving west the town thrived and old George's business grew along with it. One of his sons became a pastor and started a Baptist Church in the rapidly growing community.

Throughout the generations, the Jackson family followed the Lord and faithfully served Him. The church which had been founded by Thomas Jackson, grandson of George, stood throughout the centuries. Several times the old building had been renovated but it still remained strong until it was eventually closed down by the NWO. Since then it had been made over into a public museum which displayed UN flags, artifacts and history books filled with NWO propaganda. The NWO had its own religion which was a mixture of secular humanism, atheism, and agnosticism along with a smattering of New Age occultism. No other religion was allowed, especially Christianity and Judaism.

Reverend Jackson often thought about that old church but he was happy to be able to conduct services in his home. Bibles as well as books deemed inappropriate by the NWO had long been confiscated and destroyed.

The NWO bible depicted Jesus as a mere man, a sinner like everyone else. It was filled with false fables that blasphemed God and His Son. Jesus was made out to be the out-of-wedlock son of a poor woman called Mary who had an illicit affair with a carpenter by the name of Joseph. According to this "bible" Jesus was a disobedient boy who frequently hid from His parents in the Temple in order to avoid punishment. As a man, he led a gang of Jewish zealots in an attempt to overthrow the Roman government and drive the Romans out of Jerusalem. He was loved by the people who believed He had come to set them free from their cruel conquerors. Jesus agreed to become their king and He was about to be coronated when He was arrested. After that He was tried and crucified as a criminal. His body was put in a tomb to remain there to this day.

Of course Reverend Jackson and his little congregation knew better than to believe this propaganda. They knew the truth; Jesus was born of a virgin and was the Son of God who died on a cross in order to redeem all who came to Him in faith. They knew Jesus rose from the tomb on the third day. He had defeated

Satan and cleared the way for everyone who believed in Him to come to God and receive eternal life. God displayed His awesome love by giving His only son to die in order to open the way for man to have fellowship with Him.

Reverend Jackson was dressed in a suit and tie as he stood in his small pulpit. He always dressed like that on Sundays because he believed it honored God. The threadbare suit he wore was the only one he owned. He couldn't afford to buy a new one so he always shopped for his clothing at a thrift store. His sermons were eloquent and powerful and these made up for his lack in worldly possessions. People were so caught up in his messages they were oblivious to everything else around them.

After the service, Matilda Jackson, the reverend's wife left for the kitchen and soon reentered the parlor with cookies and a steaming pot of coffee. The people smiled as they helped themselves to the refreshments. Soon the room was filled with pleasant conversation and an occasional burst of laughter.

"When is your baby due?" a lady asked Matilda.

"Next month," Matilda beamed, her hand stroking her swollen belly. The baby complimented Matilda's loving pats with a sharp kick.

"Oh!" Matilda exclaimed with a laugh.

"What are you going to name the baby?" a man asked Reverend Jackson.

"We have been thinking about naming it Theodore if it's a boy and Theodora if it's a girl," Reverend Jackson mused.

"Awwww! I like that name." Several people smiled and nodded in agreement.

A knock was heard at the door. Reverend Jackson opened it and there stood his lifelong buddy, Pastor William White.

"Come in! Come in!" Reverend Jackson exclaimed with enthusiasm, his broad smile displaying a perfect set of straight white teeth. As he looked at his friend, Pastor White's mind traveled back to his own childhood. Many hours were spent playing with Hobart who lived just a couple of blocks away. William had been raised in a NWO orphanage ever since his parents were arrested and taken away by the NEWOPS (New World Order Police).

By this time the NWO had taken over the police stations in most of the larger cities of the nation. The NEWOPS were cruel and sadistic. They would arrest entire families and savagely beat the men before sending them off to a FEMA labor camp. The NEWOP men would often take the women to use as their pleasure slaves for a week or two before sending them to another camp far away from their husbands.

At the orphanage William was forced to attend CTE (Civic Training Exercises) for an hour twice a day. One afternoon when he was outside for his exercise period, William saw young Hobart standing outside the fence. Day after day Hobart would be waiting there for him. Finally William went up to the fence and began talking to him. Soon they became friends. William wanted to be with his new friend and play with him so he looked for a way to escape the orphanage for a few hours every day. Finally he discovered a hole in the fence and off he went to enjoy several hours of fun with Hobart.

Since Hobart lived only a couple of blocks away, he took William home with him to meet his parents. His father was a pastor and his mother was a stay-at-home Mom. Hobart had six brothers and sisters, all of whom were older than he was. Sometimes William would spend the night with Hobart. He discovered that the director of the orphanage didn't really miss him nor did he really care. The facility had become overcrowded so the discipline had become lax. Several children had escaped the facility and were now living on the streets.

4

William loved Hobart's family. Everybody was always friendly and polite and although the food was plain there was always plenty of it. One day he was invited to stay permanently with the Jackson family. He remained there until he was 18-years-old. During this time he felt a calling of God to become a pastor. Since he was unable to get a formal education he studied with Hobart's father and received a degree through him. After that he formed his own house church.

William was still daydreaming about his past when a large hand grabbed his and jarred him back to the present.

Pastor White's close set blue eyes, sharp nose and platinum blond hair betrayed his Scandinavian ancestry. He had a slight build but his large heart made up for his small size. "I came to warn you all," Pastor White breathed. "I have heard rumors that the NEWOPS are starting to arrest people in this area."

"But there hasn't been any trouble around here for years, not since the arrests that took place years ago when you were a small boy. They have left this part of the country pretty much alone," Reverend Jackson objected. "The trouble has mostly been on the East and West coasts and in the big cities."

"I heard that several house churches were raided in Kansas City and they are moving this way," Pastor White warned, lifting his index finger to scratch the point of his nose and smooth his sparse mustache. "You need to move to a safer place, a small town perhaps."

Reverend Jackson smiled and responded, "We have lived here all our lives. My father and grandfather pastored this church. We don't want to just up and leave here. We must trust God to protect us. Now why don't you sit down and have some coffee and cookies with us." After straightening his tie, he reached into his jacket pocket and drew out a large white handkerchief to wipe the perspiration off his forehead, his white teeth sparkling in a radiant smile.

Pastor White reluctantly sat in a folding chair near the door. "Perhaps it is just rumors and there is nothing to it. I hope so any way." But his face still showed apprehension as he continued to play with his mustache.

"We will be just fine." Reverend Jackson's beaming smile was contagious and Pastor White finally broke out in a grin. The conversation soon settled on the topic of the Jackson's coming baby and the room was once again filled with friendly chatter.

Chapter Two

Theodora

Several months had passed and Matilda had given birth to a beautiful baby girl. True to their word, the Jacksons named her Theodora. Because of the growing tension in the area the White family hadn't been able to visit the Jacksons to see the new baby. Everybody was staying away from crowded places as much as possible. Others were afraid to leave their homes at all.

Pastor White still conducted services in the home of his mother, Adeline White. She was a widow with two sons, William and Wilbur. After their father had passed away, they moved close by where they could keep a close eye on their mother. Pastor White had never married but Wilbur was married to a lovely woman named Edna. Wilbur and Edna had begged Adeline to come live with them but she refused. "I have my things just the way I want them. Besides I don't want to be a bother to anybody," Adeline objected. No amount of wheedling could change her mind so they finally gave up and entrusted her safety to the Lord.

It was a Saturday and Pastor White was nervously pacing the floor at his mother's house. "I am very concerned about Hobart and Matilda. I am going to take a trip over there," Pastor White decided.

"Oh please don't go over there, Will," Adeline begged. "It is just too dangerous. I heard that a family had been arrested near there the other day. Just wait here until things settle down a little more."

Pastor White lived next door to his mother so it was fairly safe to go back and forth from there. But it wasn't safe to travel any further, not even to the stores. There was a small neighborhood store, however, that was very close by and they could get milk and bread and other daily necessities there. No one dared go downtown these days.

Now Pastor White was in an argument with his mother whether or not to visit the Jackson residence.

"I will be careful, Mom. I must go and see if everybody is ok," Pastor White insisted. "I haven't heard from them in a week and I am concerned. Besides now is the best time to go. It has quieted down some the last day or so and I need to go now before things get stirred up again." With his mother still begging him to stay, he slipped out the door to begin his long trek by foot. Although he was one of the few people blessed enough to have a car, he chose to walk rather than drive the distance. A vehicle was noisy and would attract too much attention. The streets were practically devoid of automobiles these days as most people were afraid to venture out except when it was absolutely necessary.

It was a particularly muggy, hot day and the sweat dripped down Pastor White's face as he trudged along. The air was so stale and still that not a leaf on either bush or tree moved. The trip seemed to last forever and the feeling of foreboding grew deeper as he neared the Jackson residence. Within a block, he detected the stench of death that permeated the atmosphere. Pastor White quickened his pace and the pounding of his heart matched that of his racing feet. The muscles around his larynx tightened until he thought he would choke as he stepped onto the porch of the Jackson home.

On the porch he paused and took several deep agonizing breaths before placing a sweaty hand on the doorknob. He hesitated to turn it for fear of what he would see on the other side.

"Dear Jesus, please help!" he cried, his pleas rising up towards Heaven. At last he turned the knob with a trembling hand and the door opened to reveal a gut-wrenching sight.

Pastor White covered his eyes and cried out again, "Dear God, help me." His stomach churned as he observed bodies which were strewn all over the room. The pulpit that Reverend Jackson always used had been turned over on the floor in an apparent break-in. As he looked around the room he recognized the body of his dear friend lying across a sofa, his head bent down toward the floor with his feet resting on the back of the divan. He had bullet wounds in his arms, legs, and chest. Matilda's bullet riddled body rested under that of her husband's. Apparently the reverend had tried to protect his dear wife from the savage onslaught that had ensued. Bodies of parishioners who had been gunned down were scattered everywhere across the room. Blood splattered the walls and ceiling along with pools of blood on the floor. It had been an utter massacre. "Hobart! Hobart! What have they done to you? What have they done?" Deep convulsing sobs erupted from Pastor White's diaphragm as he stood there in the middle of the room. It had been nearly a week since the massacre and the bodies hadn't been discovered until now. "Why God? Oh why...why...why?"

Pastor White's groans and sobs were interrupted by a wail. He looked up to see where the sound was coming from. He listened intently in an effort to trace it but it was now silent in the house. After a couple of minutes of waiting, he heard the wailing again. It seemed to be coming from a room upstairs. Pastor White stood up and began running up the stairs, taking them two and three at a time. By now, he recognized the sound as crying and it was coming from an infant. He entered one of the bedrooms to find a crib and there lay five-month-old Theodora. Pastor White gathered the baby in his arms, wrapped her in her

9

blanket and carried her back downstairs. He began searching around for diapers, bottles, and milk. Finding a diaper bag, he gathered the baby's blankets together and carried them along with Theodora back towards Adeline's house.

As Pastor White was walking along with the precious bundle in his arms, anger began to well up inside him. He was entertaining murderous thoughts towards the NEWOPS when a quiet inner voice began to speak to him. "No! This isn't the way. I have a plan. You must trust me." Pastor White's anger began to dwindle and a supernatural sense of peace took its place. "Forgive me, Lord," he whispered.

Soon Pastor White stepped into his mother's house. "What do you have?" Adeline inquired.

"The Jackson baby," Pastor White answered.

"What? Why? What happened?" Adeline's voice quivered with alarm.

"They were...were all murdered," Pastor White stammered.

"Oh no! Tell me what happened. What happened?" Adeline's voice rose, her countenance displaying disbelief.

"It was horrible. I don't want to talk about it. Besides you wouldn't want to hear it. They were killed. Let's just leave it at that," Pastor White answered.

Adeline was in tears. "This is so awful," she cried. "This poor baby…. She has nobody now, no one to care for her." Adeline lifted her apron to wipe her eyes. "Oh, William, she must be half starved and we don't have any milk for her."

"Wait a minute," Pastor White remarked as he fumbled through the diaper bag. "Maybe there is something in here." Sure enough, he ran across two bottles tucked away in a pocket of the bag and a big can of formula at the bottom. He pulled it out and smiled. "The Lord does provide, doesn't he."

10

Adeline quickly took it to the sink and filled the bottle with water along with some of the formula. After heating it up on the stove, she gave it to Theodora who gobbled it down.

"Oh, you precious little thing," Adeline cooed, looking down at the baby adoringly.

"We must look after her," she continued. "We are all she has now." Thrusting her own feelings aside, she continued to feed Theodora and smiling at her. The baby stopped nursing long enough to flash a smile back at her with the same broad grin her father had displayed so often.

"You know something, Mom," Pastor White said. "This baby shouldn't even be alive. She went for nearly a week without any food or water. It's a miracle that she is still alive. Theodora was supernaturally protected. I believe God must have spared her for some purpose. He must have a plan for her, some great plan for the future. Else she wouldn't still be here."

"I agree," Adeline affirmed. "This child is definitely set apart for a reason. I wonder what she will turn out to be – some great leader maybe." As she mused over this thought, she lifted her eyebrows and smiled knowingly.

Adeline didn't fully understand the meaning of what she just said nor could she fathom what God's plan would be. It was one that would gradually unfold many, many years into the future, not to be fulfilled until after she had passed on from this earth; a day when Theodora would play an enormous part in God's order of events.

Chapter Three

Crisis

Four years passed and Pastor White had legally adopted Theodora. She had grown in both beauty and stature. She was going to be tall, just like her birth father. Her demeanor was angelic and she displayed unusual intelligence and wisdom for her age. Adeline was very happy to have her staying there in her home as the child was great company for her. Pastor White had signed the adoption papers shortly after taking Theodora in and Adeline had requested that the child live with her. This kept the loneliness away from both of them and it also allowed Pastor White the freedom to continue with his pastoral duties.

When Reverend Jackson had been alive he had agreed with Pastor White that Sunday services should be held at different times. Reverend Jackson would have his services in the morning while Pastor White would conduct services in the afternoon. This was done in order to avoid suspicious eyes. Pastor White held his services around 4:00 PM on Sunday afternoons at his mother's house. During those days the house churches in that area hadn't come under too much scrutiny by the government but caution was always on everyone's mind.

Ever since the brutal murders of the Jacksons and their little congregation that horrible Sunday morning, Pastor White decided extra caution was needed. He instructed the people to start coming for the Sunday services at different times beginning two hours before the meeting. Only one or two people at a time were to arrive at the house.

Although no physical copies of the Bible were available anymore, Adeline made sure that Theodora learned the teachings of Jesus and the Apostles. She would feed scripture verses to the child from memory, verses she had memorized as a child.

In years past when there were threats of Bibles being confiscated, Christian parents everywhere made it a point to memorize as much of the Holy Word as possible so they could pass it on to their children. When the government police grabbed all the Bibles, Christians were prepared. They made it a habit of coming together and pooling their resources. One after another each would share Bible verses which were recalled while another person would write the scriptures down on a pad of paper. This practice was maintained throughout the years and many hand-written New Testaments and portions of the Old Testament had been hidden away in crawl spaces, attics, and basements all over the country. In this way God's Word was preserved, fulfilling the promise that His Word would never pass away.

"Theodora, have you memorized the Bible verse I gave you this morning?" Adeline asked. It was early evening and the two had finished their supper. They had finished their nightly routine of doing the dishes; Adeline would wash and Theodora would wipe and stack them carefully on the counter for her grandmother to put away.

"Yes, Grandma, I have! Would you like me to recite it for you now?" Theodora looked up at Adeline with her large brown eyes and the corners of her mouth turned up in her usual angelic smile.

"Go ahead," Adeline smiled. Theodora obediently recited the verse from the gospel of Mark. She loved God's Word and it was no trouble for her to memorize it. In fact her sharp mind enabled her to learn very quickly and easily.

Adeline tucked Theodora in her bed and kissed her goodnight. Then she settled in her rocking chair to read from one of the books somebody had smuggled to her. Books that weren't allowed by the government were very hard to come by. But after the confiscation of the Bibles many Christians feared good books they cherished would be taken too so they hid them away over the years.

It wasn't long when black markets sprung up all over, places where people could come and purchase them. The volumes were very rare, however, making them very difficult to find. These markets were usually held at night in somebody's private home in a cellar and sometimes in the back of a Christian business building well out of the sight of the government surveillance teams. Each book had been inserted into a sleeve with a different title printed on it so as to hide its true identity. In this way, people were able to enjoy the literary works of C. S. Lewis along with many other Christian authors.

Adeline was in the middle of "The Screwtape Letters" when she heard coughing and crying coming from Theodora's bedroom. She hurried into the room to find the child flushed and burning up with fever. The thermometer revealed a temperature of 105 degrees. "Oh, dear God!" Adeline exclaimed. In a flash, she was on the telephone with the doctor.

When the doctor came and checked Theodora over, he had some grim news for Adeline. "This child has bacterial pneumonia. 50 years ago this wouldn't have been a problem but it is next to impossible to get penicillin anymore." The doctor was right. A few years after health care had become socialized, a government health board was put in place. Because of the shortage of drugs and doctors to meet the demands of the growing population, health care was rationed. The elderly, the very young, Christians and Jews were the first to be denied the life giving care. Antibiotics became nearly impossible to attain.

Adeline got on the phone and called everyone in Pastor White's church. Soon Pastor White and several people in the congregation filled Adeline's living room. Urgent prayer was lifted up to Heaven as people pled for the life of little Theodora.

"Lord, You said You had a plan for Theodora," Pastor White reminded God. "I can't believe that you would allow it to end like this. We need a miracle, Lord. Without penicillin the doctor said there is little chance that she will survive. Please, God....oh, dear God!" Along with the others, he prayed most of the night.

Theodora's breathing became labored. The doctor stayed with her and fed her oxygen through a mask which was attached to a small tank he had brought with him. Fortunately oxygen was still available because it was used for many purposes.

The child's temperature continued to rise and she began to go into convulsions. Her entire body trembled and shook violently. Her eyes were rolled back in her head and saliva drooled from her mouth. Pastor White stood in the doorway of her room and observed everything that was happening. He fell on his knees and began sobbing. "O God, please....please!" he moaned. He paused and looked up and then continued, "I believe. Please help me trust You more, Father."

"You need to get some sleep," the doctor said. "There is nothing here you can do. If there is any change I will let you know."

It was 5:00 AM when all the people had left and Pastor White reluctantly crawled into his bed. Adeline was still downstairs fast asleep in her rocking chair.

Pastor White fell into a fitful sleep. He began to dream of dark images, black creatures that were flying around Theodora's bed. They were tugging at her and trying to drag her away. "Leave her alone," Pastor White screamed. Suddenly the room was filled with a bright light and he heard a voice saying, "Trust me. I have a plan." Pastor White jerked awake, his wide eyes

15

staring and looking around. Was it a dream? Did he hear a voice? He couldn't be sure. He looked at his watch and it was 8:00 AM.

A knock sounded outside his door and it slowly opened. It was the doctor. He looked haggard and solemn.

"O God, no! Noooo!" Pastor White cried to himself. His heart was in his throat and he felt numb all over as he braced himself for bad news. Then he detected a weary smile playing at the corners of the doctor's mouth.

"She will be just fine," he assured.

Pastor White breathed a sigh of relief. "O ye of little faith!" he thought.

"Her fever broke a few minutes ago and her lungs are showing signs of clearing. Her breathing isn't as labored now," the doctor continued. "She just needs plenty of bed rest, fluids and nourishment. I don't know what happened. Just when I thought I was going to lose her she began to rally. I can't explain it."

"I can," Pastor White remarked with a telling smile. Here was a perfect opportunity to share the gospel of Jesus and His healing power with the physician.

Chapter Four

First Day at School

Adeline brushed Theodora's thick black hair until it shined. The girl had turned five-years-old six months ago. Now she was getting ready for her first day at school. Her pinafore dress hung in the closet all pressed and ready and Theodora was excited to put it on.

"Grandma, what is school like?" she asked flashing a big toothy grin with a space in the middle. She hadn't reached the age of losing her baby teeth yet. It happened one day when she had gotten too rambunctious at play and fell. She hit her mouth on the edge of a table and one of her front teeth came flying out. A visit to the doctor revealed she had no real injuries. He gave her a lollipop and promised Theodora that her tooth would grow back, just a little later than usual. After that she proudly showed all her playmates the space where her tooth used to be.

Adeline sat down and held Theodora on her lap. "You will learn a lot of things that aren't true," she explained. "You mustn't pay any attention to anything you hear at school. Just concentrate on your math and reading. Remember that anything you hear or read that doesn't agree with the Word of God must be ignored. Satan will try to fool you with his silly lies."

Throughout Theodora's young life, Adeline tried to explain to her about the Bible and how everybody once had a written copy of it. "Satan hates the Bible and he hates Jesus and Christians. This is why the enemy took our Bible away from us. But he can't take it out of our hearts. He can never steal the truth from us as long as we stay close to Jesus. You must always remember that, Theodora."

Theodora alternatively walked and skipped all the way to school. She wondered what new friends she would make. She also hoped that she would meet other Christian girls and boys she could play with.

When Theodora arrived in the classroom she was confronted with a stern looking teacher, Miss Potter. She never smiled and her eyes were as grey as her personality. Looking at her gave Theodora a creepy feeling.

Things weren't as much fun as the girl had anticipated. It was more like a boot camp than a school. There were two one hour periods of CTE which were held both in the morning and afternoon; only a small amount of math and reading was taught. The emphasis was always on the NWO and its propaganda; why they believe the way they do and how it is good for everybody to follow their rules. After all they know best, better than parents, the students were taught.

An enormous picture of the World President hung on a wall and the New World flag stood by the right side of the teacher's desk. It was amazingly similar to the Nazi flag that flew all over Germany so very long ago. But this one had three black sixes in the center instead of the swastika. As she looked at it, Theodora knew it stood for something bad. Her grandmother had warned her about all the lies and propaganda she would hear at school.

When Theodora grew old enough, her grandmother would tell her things she would be able to understand. She would tell her about the Third Reich and the horrible Jewish holocaust. Theodora would learn about the World Wars and the heroes who saved the country and many others by defeating evil regimes like Hitler, Stalin and Mussolini.

Of course none of this was ever taught at school. The truth had been eradicated from all the history books and replaced with myths that complied with the NWO propaganda. Students learned that the NWO was a great organization that had to be set up in order to bring in world peace, a Utopia that had long since been in the planning. These students would never learn about Hitler's cruel dictatorship; how he had the Jews thrown into gas chambers to be killed and then their bodies burned in ovens that belched smoke day and night.

Right now all Theodora understood was that her grandmother always told her the truth about God and how much He loved her. He wanted everyone everywhere to come to Him and become His friend.

Theodora's mind was protected from the lies of the devil because her father and grandmother along with her aunt and uncle prayed for her every day. They made sure she learned the truth by teaching her what really had happened in America from the time of its inception right up until now. They repeatedly taught her in simple ways that a six-year-old could understand.

In her little way of sharing the love of Jesus with others, Theodora would often draw pictures of Jesus and stick them into the doorways of neighbor's houses. She would make Him smiling so people would know He loved them. Now as she sat in school, she was thinking about all the things she had learned at home when the teacher called her name.

"Theodora, are you paying attention? This is very important so you must pay attention," Miss Potter scolded. Theodora sat up straight and pretended to listen; but she had learned to shut out the constant torrent of humanistic propaganda because she knew it wasn't the truth. She had been taught at home to only listen to truth and hold Jesus close to her heart.

Kindergarten was in session for a full day six days of the week. There was no recess and lunch period lasted only a half

19

hour. Nobody was allowed to bring lunches from home. Students were allowed to eat only the government approved food. No child was overweight because of the low calorie menus.

During the time when recess had ordinarily taken place years ago there was a half hour of rigorous exercise and calisthenics each morning and afternoon. Most of the children were malnourished due to the unsubstantial lunches but Theodora was rigorous and in good health. Her grandmother made sure she got a good nourishing hot breakfast before school and more healthy snacks along with a nice hot supper afterward. Most parents were both working and had no time to fix good meals. Their children picked around at whatever they could find while waiting for them to return home from work. Like most of them typically do, they feasted on junk food.

For most children, school began at the age of three. Parents were both forced to work in order to provide for the ever rising cost of living. There wasn't anybody left to babysit so they were forced to place their children in government run preschools. This had been cleverly planned many years earlier. The government bureaucrats knew that the earlier they could start indoctrinating children to their world view the easier it would be to create more people after their own kind.

This line of reasoning had been introduced by the Communists. By the time students would graduate, they would be completely transformed into world citizens who were in lock step with the NWO. Pastor White and Adeline made sure this wouldn't happen to Theodora so they continued to pump her with the truth of the Bible along with lots of prayer.

After the regular school period a time was set aside for the children to play until they were dismissed for the day. One afternoon Theodora noticed a girl in her class standing in the schoolyard alone, apart from the other children. She went up to her to introduce herself and soon discovered that she was a Christian too. Happily they began playing together and talking about their home lives. They wondered if they were the only Christians at that school. It was difficult to find out because it wasn't wise to reveal who you were if you were a follower of Jesus. Theodora had been warned about that.

"It is never safe to let others know who you are," Adeline warned.

"But how can we tell people about Jesus?" Theodora asked.

"We have to trust the Holy Spirit to show us who to talk to and when it is safe," Adeline said.

It was like this when Theodora had first spotted Heather that day. She saw in her eyes the same look so many Christians had. Being sensitive to the voice of the Holy Spirit, Theodora knew it was safe to talk to her. "This one is ok," God seemed to say. That was when Theodora had approached her. The pair of girls walked home together, hand in hand. Theodora discovered that Heather lived in the next block.

"Grandma, guess what!" she exclaimed with exuberance as she ran through the door.

"What is that?" Adeline smiled. She lay the dishtowel down and gathered Theodora in her arms for a big grandma hug.

"I found a new friend." She wrapped her arms around Adeline's neck and gave her a kiss on the cheek.

Chapter Five

The Topeka Home Groups

Pastor White had been appointed as the lead pastor over all the home groups of the Baptist Churches located in the city of Topeka. This kept him very busy but he found the time to lead the group that met regularly in the home of Adeline White.

Ever since the massacre that had occurred at the Jackson residence, things had quieted down in the city so Sunday and Wednesday night meetings resumed as usual. Extra caution had been taken of course. Each home where the meetings took place had been renovated with secret basement rooms that were assessable through undetectable doors. Sometimes false cabinet shelves were built in front of the doors with tools, appliances, and other accessories piled on top. These were made to open up to the hidden doors through which believers could pass into the secret rooms in an emergency. In other houses false closets led to the doors and into the rooms through them.

People would still come to the meetings one or two at a time, spread apart over a two hour period. Baptist pastors were given secret codes for the parishioners, a special knock to use on the doors of meeting places so the host or hostess inside would recognize it as belonging to one of them. People were warned not to answer their doors unless they heard that knock.

By this time most of the churches in the city had been compromised and were now part of the New World Council of Churches. Most of the evangelical and full gospel churches remained true to the Lord. It was only these churches which had been closed down and turned into schools, museums, or meeting halls of the NWO. The NEWOPS hadn't caused any more trouble for the last few years so believers in the city became more relaxed and even a little careless.

"The snake is still coiled in silence ready to strike when you would least expect," Pastor White warned. At the monthly meetings with the other Baptist clergy in town much prayer for guidance and protection was lifted up.

At one of these meetings, the Lord spoke to Pastor White. "I want my church united." Pastor White looked up at the other pastors in the meeting room and began to share God's plan.

"God wants all true believers to join together. We need to invite members of other churches who are true to the faith to join us. We should include the pastors of these other denominations in our meetings."

The other Baptist pastors agreed. United the church would be much stronger against the enemy. So an invitation went out to several other churches in the community. Many new faces appeared at the next meeting. The new pastors were introduced to the plan. They learned how to protect their parishioners through secret codes, passages, and hiding places.

In the mean time Satan was very angry. He had plans of his own.

The NEWOPS were getting ready to strike again. It was an opportune time because the people had grown complacent and wasn't paying much attention to what was happening around them.

Pastor White spoke up at one of the meetings. "I am very concerned about the attitude of the people. They are beginning to be nonchalant and careless about where they are going and what they are doing. Some of them are falling back into worldly ways and getting caught up in the lies of the enemy."

The other pastors nodded in agreement. "Perhaps we need to talk about this more in our meetings," a pastor suggested.

"The emphasis has been on prayer and how much God has blessed us and prayer is good but we need to put caution with them. Wisdom is needed. People need to be reminded that there are consequences to every action."

"Yes!" another piped up. "Proverbs is a good place to start. They are full of wisdom and a good guide for the people."

After the meeting, the pastors followed through and began teaching the people the deeper ways of God. At his next Sunday meeting, Pastor White stood up before everyone and began his sermon.

"We can't be too careless in our walk with God. Some of you and you know who you are have been neglecting your time with Him. You have even fallen back into some of your old ways before you gave your life to Jesus. I must warn you that when you do this, your spiritual ears and eyes grow dim. You aren't able to hear when the Holy Spirit speaks to you. Satan goes about like a hungry lion seeking whom he may devour. In other words, he is always on the move to deceive people. When you neglect God, the propaganda of the NWO begins to sound pretty good, enticing in fact."

Pastor White paused, wiped his forehead with a handkerchief and then continued. "I know you don't want to hear this because this is a hard word; but I love you and God has commissioned me to always tell you the truth whether it is pleasant to hear or not. I don't want to be one of those who just tickle your ears. That is what a false shepherd does. I haven't been called to do that."

As the people listened some of them broke down in tears and knelt down on the floor. Others fell prostrate. "Father, please forgive me," a man prayed. Pastor White laid his hands first on one and then another as people repented on their faces before the Lord.

"I have often fallen short in my walk with Jesus too," Pastor White admitted. "That word was just as much for me as it was for you. We need to always be on our guard, daily putting on our spiritual armor of prayer and the Word of God."

When everybody had gone home after the service, Adeline smiled and said, "Thank you, son, for that word. It surely was a message from the Lord. I have noticed that the Holy Spirit hasn't been moving as much lately at our meetings and now I know why. I thank God for you, that you were able to pick up on that and then obey God with that message."

"I felt a strong conviction to do so and now I am glad I did," the pastor said. "Now why don't we get a cup of coffee before we enjoy our supper?"

Chapter Six

Wednesday Night Bible Study

Several months went by and the Holy Spirit was moving in both services. People had heeded the word Pastor White had given on that particular Sunday. As a result the group grew and another home had to be opened in order to accommodate all the people. One of the pastor's associates, who was studying to become a minister, led the other one.

It was Wednesday night and Adeline White was busy in the kitchen getting ready for the meeting in her home. She had on the flowered apron she always wore when preparing food or refreshments. Her hair was neatly pinned up in a bun with combs which contained little beads that resembled pearls. She whistled a certain favorite hymn of hers as she was working. Coffee was perking on the stove as she removed a hot pan of cookies from the oven. Theodora who was now 7 years old was helping her. She had on her favorite pinafore dress she always wore to meetings. It was the only dress she owned. Most people didn't have a very large wardrobe because they were poor and had to live modestly. Likewise meals were plain but they were ample for the most part.

Just as Adeline had finished up in the kitchen, a coded knock was heard at the door. "Would you go answer that please, Theodora?" Adeline asked politely.

"Sure, Grandma," Theodora replied as she headed towards the door. She opened it and Evelyn Walker stepped into the living room. She was a middle aged lady who had never married. Her slightly graying hair was worn in a short bob and she was casually dressed in a pair of jeans and turtle neck sweater.

Evelyn was raised in a godly family so she was fluent in the Bible. Adeline utilized her as one of her mainstays when recording Bible verses during the meetings. Though Evelyn had a strong faith, she could be rather judgmental at times towards some of the others at the meeting. It was difficult for her to relate to some of their problems and hang-ups due to the fact that she had come from such a straight-laced background.

For example, Evelyn had a difficult time accepting John Sommers. He had come out of the homosexual life style and it took a while for her to recognize that God had delivered him from that sin.

Then there was Alice. She had been a drug addict and would steal in order to feed her habit before she met Christ. At first Evelyn wondered if she had really changed and she viewed her rather suspiciously at times.

Because of Pastor White's teachings, Evelyn's judgmental nature had tempered over the years. She now was able to receive others with genuine love. Evelyn learned that it wasn't her job to change them so she was now willing to allow the Holy Spirit to do that job. He was the only One who could change people's hearts and attitudes. Jesus was in the business of saving people, not Evelyn. Her job was simply to love and accept people as they were. When she did this she discovered that she earned the right to share the truth of the gospel with others; and by doing so with love, they were willing to listen.

Over the next two hours, people came. Paul and Martha Betzler were the last couple to arrive and they were accompanied by their children. Paul came with his two sons first and a half hour later Martha joined him along with their two daughters. Paul owned a gas station and was able to fully support his wife and children so Martha could be a stay-at-home Mom. Paul had a secret cubby hole in a back room at the gas station where he hid away forbidden books out from under the nose of the NWO.

Lastly Pastor White arrived and the small group of people was soon prepared for the meeting to begin. Those with children had brought them one or two at a time just as the Betzlers had done. As soon as everyone was seated and ready, Pastor White took out his little tablet with the handwritten gospel of John and set it on the podium that had been brought up from the cellar.

After opening prayer, the pastor began to teach. Meanwhile the children had followed Uncle Wilbur and Aunt Edna into the secret room in the basement to hear their favorite Bible stories. Theodora's favorite story was that of the Good Samaritan. She often thought of her father as being one. He never hesitated to reach out to hurting people and invite them to the house for a meal. Soon he won them over to the Lord and they started attending the church services in their house. Because of the anticipation of hearing what Pastor White had to share, nobody noticed that there was one missing.

Chapter Seven

Anna

It was 7:00 PM when Anna left her house to attend the Wednesday night Bible study at Adeline's house. She was a teenager, only sixteen years old and her parents thought she was going over to her friend's house to study. The girl carried her book bag with her to give them that impression. Her parents weren't believers so they were compliant with the ways of the NWO. Both worked outside the home so were away a lot but when they were at home they loved throwing parties during which there was a lot of drinking, filthy jokes and coarse language taking place.

Anna was only too glad to get away from that atmosphere because the Holy Spirit within her was grieved by everything that happened in that home. Marlene, her best friend, was a Christian and so were her parents. Anna liked hanging out there because she felt safe and clean. So whenever she went to the Wednesday night Bible studies her parents assumed she was with Marlene. They didn't seem to mind or care where Anna went any way. Most of the time, they were intoxicated with either alcohol, marijuana or some other drug.

Tonight, Anna was wearing a heavy coat as it was cold outside. Snow lay on the ground and a full moon shining down on the bare trees cast long shadows over the pale landscape. Her boots crunched in the snow as she walked the eight blocks towards Adeline's home. There was something rather eerie about this night and Anna had a very discomforting feeling about it. As she trudged along the premonition grew within her until she wondered if she should turn back.

She thought about Marlene who was in attendance at the Wednesday night service in her home. Marlene's father was a lay pastor who headed up the meetings there. Her house was closer than the White residence so she thought about going over there. But then again, she would be missed by Adeline and the others. Besides she didn't want to skip the teaching Pastor White would be sharing that night.

A commotion could be heard a block away. Anna stopped in her tracks to listen. "What is it?" she wondered. She started walking towards the sound and was soon able to see what was going on. The NEWOPS were back and they were forcing themselves into people's houses. There were some gun shots along with terrified screams. The police were dragging people from their homes, and pulling out some of the women by their hair.

Anna tried to run but she couldn't get her feet and legs to move. It was like one of those nightmares when she was being chased. She would try to move but her feet were glued to the ground.

It dawned on Anna that the NWO had discovered the homes where the believers met in secret. People were now being arrested everywhere. They were being hauled away to prison and being tortured in order to force information out of them. The NEWOPS were seeking the names and addresses of other believers as well as the places where they would meet. Some people, due to the duress and aguish of being tortured, gave them the information they desired. This was probably why this raid was now taking place in Topeka. Someone in another town had given the NEWOPS what they wanted.

Anna's throat tightened in fear and a cold chill went through her body as she tried to think of what to do. She knew that she had to hurry and warn everybody. But how would she keep from getting caught? She decided she would keep out of sight by walking across the backyards of homes. Some of the houses had fenced in yards so she had to weave in and out in order to stay safely out of sight.

As Anna was walking cautiously along something in the distance caught her eye. She inched ahead until she was close enough to see what or who it was. When she could make it out she stopped and stood frozen with fear; it was a NEWOP. Her heart jumped inside her.

"What am I going to do?" Anna thought to herself. She looked this way and that until she spotted a large oak tree. She decided it was big enough to hide behind so she quietly snuck around it and pressed her back tightly against the large trunk. The NEWOP began moving in her direction and was slowly closing in on her. She closed her eyes tightly and lifted up a prayer of desperation.

"Help me, Lord!" Anna cried to herself. She scarcely breathed for fear the policeman would hear her. Anna opened her eyes long enough to see him creeping up on her. Before she knew it, he was looking straight at her.

"I've been caught," Anna thought, terror shooting like electricity through her entire body. She winced and closed her eyes tightly. Suddenly there was a flash of light, so bright that she could see it through her closed eyelids.

"What was that?" she wondered. When she opened her eyes there was no policeman, absolutely nobody anywhere to be seen. Had she imagined it all? She didn't dare move though.

Anna prayed and looked around and then prayed some more. She saw that the police cars were still there and she was afraid the NEWOP would return to nab her. It seemed like an eternity passed before the NEWOPS finally returned to their cars.

Anna was able to breathe easier but she didn't step out from behind the tree until she was absolutely sure they were all gone.

As Anna walked by the ravaged houses with doors half hanging off their hinges, she shuddered knowing she hadn't imagined it all. This had been a real experience.

Anna looked at her watch and was surprised that two and a half hours had transpired. She had missed the meeting. She hurried now, hoping some of the people were still there.

While all this had been happening, Evelyn had noticed that Anna was missing from the group. She interrupted Pastor White in the middle of his teaching to voice her alarm.

"Anna isn't here," Evelyn nearly shouted. "I saw her this morning and she told me she was coming tonight. Something is wrong...terribly wrong. What are we going to do?"

"Pray!" Pastor White exclaimed. "That is all we can do. Pray and trust God." He had experienced the power of prayer many times. The Lord was aware of every detail of every life present in that room and His gentle hand was upon them. So the pastor led his little congregation in prayer as people knelt, lay headlong on the floor or just sat in their chairs with heads bowed. Everyone joined in prayer as they made their appeals to Heaven. Unknown to everyone else, this was taking place during the time that Anna had been confronted by the NEWOP. The prayer continued for an hour and then Pastor White felt a release in his spirit.

"He has answered," Pastor White assured everyone. The little group of people sensed a supernatural peace settling down over the room. "Let us return to our Bible study," Pastor White said. "Everything is going to be alright." Everybody nodded in agreement and several eyes were fastened on the door as if Anna was going to walk straight through it at any moment. And approximately two and a half hours since the meeting began, a knock was heard at the door. This time Adeline answered it and there stood Anna.

Chapter Eight

Arrested

Peals of praises filled the room as people rejoiced and hugged Anna. Everyone had questions for Anna so she told them everything that had happened. When she got to the part where she was almost caught by a NEWOP there was a hush in the room except for a few gasps. After a pause Evelyn asked, "What time was it when the NEWOP saw you?"

"I don't know what time it was but it was about an hour and a half ago in my best estimation," Anna answered.

"Then it was a miracle," Pastor White interjected. "An angel must have blinded the eyes of the NEWOP so he couldn't see you, Anna."

"But he was looking straight at me." Anna's eyes grew wide with amazement. "That must have been when I saw that flash of bright light. It must have been an angel but my eyes were shut so tightly I couldn't see him." Anna paused to think about what she just said and then remembered about the warning. "Everybody!" she shouted. "Run! They could be here any minute."

"Yes! All of you! You better go into the secret room. I will stay here," Pastor White urged. It was only two minutes later when a loud pounding was heard at the door. It wasn't the code so the pastor knew it must be the NEWOPS. Shouting came from the other side of the door. "You let us in right now," a voice bellowed.

Pastor White stood still momentarily and tried to think of what to do. He didn't want them to bust in and he didn't want the people downstairs to be put in any danger. He prayed and then decided it would be best to open the door. When he did they rushed right in. One of them had a large build and a mustache and his name was Bart. The other one, Matt, was smaller and younger with a slight build. Both were dressed in beige uniforms with the NWO insignia on their upper left sleeves. On their feet were jack boots such as the NAZIs had worn during the time of Hitler. In fact their uniforms very much resembled those of the NAZIs, the only difference being the insignia.

"Is your name William White?" Bart snarled.

"It is. What do you want with me?" came the answer.

"You are under arrest," one of the NEWOPS growled.

"For what charge?" Pastor White's voice became defiant.

The NEWOP jerked out a handbook of NWO laws and regulations. "For violating Articles 431 and 432 which state: There shall be no house meetings for the purpose of conducting religious services which are not specifically authorized by the State," he began. "All religious services must be held in buildings which have been licensed and approved by the NWO. Children under the age of 21 are forbidden to be given religious instruction other than that of the approved doctrine of the Council of World Religions. William White, you have been accused of breaking the law on these two counts. If you are found guilty by the World Court, you will be sentenced to death. What have you got to say for yourself?"

"I have nothing to say to you," Pastor White answered, his upper lip held stiffly.

"Now the World Court will surely find you guilty because of all the evidence we have against you. But if you will give us the names and addresses of those other government rebels that meet in your house, I will try to convince the Court to go easy on you," Bart promised.

"You are asking me to betray my friends and neighbors? How dare you?" Anger had slowly built up in the pastor.

35

"Well there is more than one way to get that information out of you. You will be sorry you ever defied the NWO. The execution you will be facing is both very painful and unpleasant." While Bart grabbed Pastor White's arm, Matt slapped handcuffs on his wrists.

Suddenly Theodora tore into the room from the basement. She was followed by Adeline.

"You leave my daddy alone," Theodora screamed. She began kicking Matt who protested loudly. Adeline grabbed her in an attempt to hold the child back.

"Who is this?" Bart demanded.

"This is my daughter and my mother," Pastor White answered. "My daughter is staying with my mother so she will have someone to look after her when I'm working."

"She sure doesn't look like your daughter to me," Bart sneered.

"She is adopted. Her parents were murdered by one of your people," Pastor White snarled, glaring defiantly at the NEWOPS.

"Come on! Let's go!" Bart jerked Pastor White by the arm.

"Can I have a minute to talk to my daughter?" Pastor White pleaded.

"Alright but make it snappy. We ain't got all day," Bart groused.

Pastor White gathered Theodora in his arms and began speaking gently to her. "Now I want you to listen closely to me, Theodora. Remember that no matter what happens God is always in control. When I first looked into your eyes after finding you alone in your crib, I saw something there, something I had never seen before. I knew then that there was something very special about you; God had a plan and you were chosen as a vessel to fulfill it.

"I don't understand, Daddy," Theodora said between sobs. "What plan is that?

"God hasn't shown me what it is, honey, but He assured me that He has one. None of us will know what it is until the right time comes. When that day arrives He will show it to you." Pastor White assured. "Remember I will always love you."

"Oh Daddy, I love you too," the little girl sobbed convulsively.

"Are you through with all this nonsense now?" Bart growled. Pastor White gave Theodora a final kiss and was led out the door in his shackles. Matt turned around and asked, "Shouldn't we arrest those two as well?"

"Just leave them be for now. We got what we came for – this big cheese troublemaker. Without him any planned rebellion in this community should fall apart," Bart answered. "We can always come back for these two later. Let's go."

As soon as the door closed, Theodora ran into her grandmother's arms and sobbed. "I won't ever see my daddy again, will I?" Theodora cried.

"No, child, but he is in our Heavenly Father's care," Adeline said softly as she patted the girl on her back and rocked her back and forth in her arms. Silent tears spilled down the old woman's face to drop on the top of Theodora's head.

Chapter Nine

Trouble Astir

Nine months had passed since the arrest and Adeline had just received some sad news concerning her son, Pastor White. He had undergone sleep deprivation, starvation, water boarding and unimaginable forms of torture at the hands of the NEWOPS. But he refused to give them any information about the people he had been shepherding over the years. Finally in frustration they took him into a room, strapped him down on a table and inoculated him with a lethal injection, declaring that he had committed the highest form of treason. Adeline was grieving but her sorrow was combined with a sense of pride. Her son had died a hero. She knew that he was in Heaven now receiving crowns for his faithfulness. Theodora had just turned eight years old now.

"I can't believe how big you have gotten to be," Adeline crowed.

Theodora nodded but had a grim expression on her face.

Noticing her downcast expression, Adeline asked, "Honey, what's the matter? What's troubling you? I know something has been bothering you lately. Now tell Grandma what it is." Adeline put her arm around the girl.

"Grandma," Theodora began. "Life just doesn't make any sense any more. If you behave at school, you are punished and if you are a brat you are rewarded. Today I was trying to be nice and help a girl with her spelling lesson and the teacher jumped all over me. I thought she would be glad I was helping her. Another kid pushed a girl down in the mud getting her dress all dirty. Everybody laughed, even the teacher. Then instead of scolding the boy who pushed her down, the teacher yelled at the girl just because she is a Christian. She told her to go home and change her clothes or she wouldn't be allowed to come back to school. I thought that was just plain mean. Everything seems to be upside down."

"That is what the Bible said it would be like in the last days just before the Lord returns," Adeline explained. "Bad would be called good and good would be called bad so we shouldn't be surprised. Besides Jesus warned His followers that they would be hated by the people in this world who don't love Him."

"I still don't know why I am here. Every day is the same and nothing ever gets any better," Theodora whined. "The only friend I have is Heather. I wish we could just go away and live somewhere else...somewhere people aren't so mean...somewhere we don't have to be afraid all the time."

"Why Theodora," Adeline scolded. "After all the times your Uncle Wilbur and Aunt Edna have told you, you still don't remember? You have been chosen by God and you have a very special reason for being here. Your father, before he was taken away, told you the same thing. How many times do you have to be told, child?"

Theodora stood, hanging her head down, and looked with big sad eyes up at her grandmother.

"It will all be ok, honey," Adeline assured, hugging Theodora to her breast. "Just remember you are loved."

Adeline hadn't told Theodora the news about her father yet. She was afraid the girl would ask about him any day and she wouldn't know what to tell her. She had been afraid to say anything. Theodora had to cope with so many things at school and Adeline didn't know if she could handle the truth. As she rolled these thoughts around in her mind over and over again she decided it was best to say nothing and just forget it. What purpose would it serve for Theodora to know? The girl had already reconciled to the fact that she would never see her father

39

again. Her thoughts turned to the present as she shared more with Theodora.

"I know it has been a difficult time for you, child," Adeline soothed. "It hasn't been easy for any of us. But we must keep on trusting Jesus, honey. There is nothing else we can do. Why don't we just hold hands and pray. We can still thank Jesus for what we do have. Most of all we can thank Him for saving us and being our Friend."

Adeline took a sip of her coffee and then continued, "People without Jesus are in much worse shape than we are even if it doesn't seem like it. We look at them and see all the 'goodies' the government has given them. But they really don't have it nearly as good as we do. What they have now is only temporary. When they die these things will all be gone. Without Jesus they will never be able to enjoy the blessings of Heaven."

"Is that right, Grandma?" Theodora said, yawning sleepily.

"Yes, Theodora, and we need to always remember to thank Jesus because He has given us a gift far greater than this world can give." With that being said, Adeline grasped Theodora's hands and they began to pray together. Theodora felt her spirits rise as they lifted up thanksgiving to the Lord. She realized then how good she really had it and she felt ashamed of herself for forgetting that.

There was a knock at the door and Adeline, recognizing the secret code, answered it. It was Uncle Wilbur.

"I just received word that the NWO has passed a new law," Uncle Wilbur said grimly.

"Now what are they up to?" Adeline asked with disgust in her voice.

"They want to rid the world of all the elderly who are over the age of 70 as well as the handicapped," Uncle Wilbur shared. "They claim they are a drain on the economy. They believe the earth can't handle the size the population has grown to be so they made plans to reduce it. They believe by euthanizing those who are less than perfect the problem will be solved."

"This sounds like the holocaust all over again," Adeline responded with both disgust and alarm in her voice. She had just finished reading all about it from an old history book. She had found it at a black market that Paul Betzler secretly held in the back room of his gas station every Thursday night. "What does this mean for us now?" she continued.

"It means that we have to get you out of here. It means we all have to move to a more secluded place where we can keep you safe. And there is no time to spare because the law came with an order for all households to give up their elderly and handicapped people. People have been threatened with imprisonment and worse if they refuse." Uncle Wilbur's facial expression showed he was quite serious.

"But how? You know if we leave here they will track us," Adeline exclaimed. Tracking devices had long since been put on all automobiles so the NWO could locate the whereabouts of every vehicle at all times.

"Paul has a mechanic working for him that is a whiz at removing these devices. I will go to the gas station right now and have him remove it. Paul and his mechanic are both there and are waiting for me. You see, I had it all planned ahead so trust me," Uncle Wilbur explained.

Wilbur grabbed the keys to his suburban and headed toward the door. "When I get back we can leave here and no one will be the wiser," he said. "Now go ahead and start packing. We can only take a few things with us so select only the things you need to get by with. By the time I return I want you and Theodora to be ready to go." Uncle Wilbur stepped into his car and Adeline watched him through the window as he turned out of the driveway and drove down the street.

"Hurry, Theodora!" Adeline urged. "Pack your suitcase with only the things you think you will need." She handed the child an old suitcase. Theodora grabbed it and began stuffing everything she could into it.

"Grandma, I can't get everything I want to take into this suitcase," Theodora cried. She had continued to cram more and more into the container until she couldn't possibly get any more in. She was crying in frustration now.

"I told you to pack only what you need," Adeline reminded. Then she put a comforting arm around the girl. "Don't fret so, child. It is only stuff. Stuff is just temporary, remember? The really important things, those that are eternal, you will carry with you always."

Theodora remembered what they had just prayed about. She dried her tears and smiled. "You are right, Grandma."

Two hours later Uncle Wilbur returned and he had Aunt Edna with him along with a suitcase she had packed. It was now dark outside. "Hurry now! It's time to go," Uncle Wilbur said.

"Where are we going?" Theodora asked.

"To Colorado," Uncle Wilbur answered, fervently jabbing a finger towards the car. "Now hurry up! We can't waste time. We have to reach the border before it gets light. It will be harder for the NEWOPS to spot us in the dark. We will take the side roads and stay away from the Interstates and main highways. I know of a border crossing that isn't patrolled. We will cross over into Colorado from there."

"How do you know all this about where to go and all?" Adeline asked.

"Paul has friends in Colorado. One of them is a Cherokee by the name of Johnny Fast Horse. Paul has been in contact with

42

him so he is expecting us. Johnny will take care of us once we get there. He stays in a cabin near Gunnison. It is quite secluded and we will be safe there," Uncle Wilbur explained.

Unbeknownst to Adeline and Theodora, Uncle Wilbur had been making plans with Paul for several months. They knew that something was in the wind. When Uncle Wilbur had sensed that something nefarious was going on with the NWO he began to prepare for the move ahead of time. He conferred with Paul who had gotten in touch with his friend so everything could be arranged in the event the family would have to move. Now with the car all packed the little family was on their way.

Chapter Ten

Journey West

It was a rough ride over many ruts, rocks, and dead tree limbs on the dirt road they were traveling on. These side roads hadn't been kept up and many of them had become nearly impassible, but this was good. They were likely to be free of squad cars and the Whites would practically have the roads to themselves. They could relax knowing there was little chance of being detected.

"I was afraid we wouldn't get out of town without being noticed," Adeline remarked.

"That is why I chose to leave when we did," Wilbur explained. "There was a big festival downtown last night and I knew that most of the NEWOPS would be stationed there to keep order. Some of them probably joined in the celebration even though it's illegal for them to drink while on duty. The NWO has been pretty lenient with them and as long as their police force keeps up with the quota of Christians and Jews they arrest, they don't bother much with disciplining their own kind. When it comes to people like us, however, it's a much different story."

Theodora had been listening to the conversation but now her eyes were growing heavy with sleep. She was curled up in the back seat with her head resting on Aunt Edna's lap when she drifted off. The occasional thumping and bumping of the vehicle didn't appear to bother her.

It seemed peculiar to the family never to see another car but they were glad. As long as they were alone they knew there would be no danger. They watched out the windows to see tractors left vacant in the fields after a hard day's work. They saw several herds of cattle standing in the fields and waved at them as they went by. It was August and very hot as could be expected in Kansas. Back home, the nights didn't cool down much from the heat during the daytimes. It was typical for the temperature to stay at 80 degrees or above all night. The city turned off the electricity around 7:00 PM each evening in order to preserve energy. Houses remained cool for a few hours after the air conditioning had been shut off but the evening sun that still remained soon warmed them back up again.

Theodora hardly noticed the heat. Children seemed to be pretty versatile when it came to the climate; neither the summer nor winter temperatures bothered them that much. However Adeline's 72-year-old body didn't adapt well to the extremes of the Kansas climate. She looked forward to the much more tolerable weather in the foothills of the Rocky Mountains where the air was drier and fresher and the nights were cool and still.

The four wheel drive suburban continued on the rough terrain for several hours. Then around 2:00 AM the engine began to wheeze and sputter. The car came to a crawl and eventually stopped.

"Please God, not now," Wilbur prayed. He got out of the vehicle and opened the hood. It was a gasket. Uncle Wilbur gave a sigh of relief. Paul had given him some extra parts for the journey just in case they might be needed before they reached their destination. A gasket that had been stowed away in the back just happened to be among them. It was less than 400 miles from Topeka to the border but the rutty roads made for a slow journey. Now this! Uncle Wilbur was concerned that they wouldn't reach the border before sunrise. He hurriedly made the necessary repairs and they were on their way again.

Unexpectedly distant headlights peeped over a hill on the road. Shock waves traveled down Wilbur's spine as he watched the rapidly approaching vehicle. He had been getting drowsy but now he was wide awake. As he watched the car draw nearer and nearer, his heart began pounding furiously in his chest. Wilbur pulled the suburban off to one side of the road and turned off the headlights. He hoped it hadn't been seen as he watched the distant car close in. Soon Wilbur was able to see that it was a squad car. He held his breath as it came to a stop next to the White's parked vehicle.

"Dear God, help us," Wilbur wheezed. The NEWOP got out of his car and started walking towards him. Wilbur remained in a frozen position in his seat. The officer motioned for him to get out of the car.

"This is it," Wilbur thought to himself. Suddenly, out of nowhere, there was a blinding flash of brilliant white light causing him to tightly close his eyes. He thought it was lightening and he listened for the thunder that was sure to follow. Moments passed and he didn't hear a thing.

Wilbur sat there for a while before daring to open his eyes again. When he did, he fully expected to see the officer with his gun pointed right at him. Instead he saw no one. In surprise he looked around, this way and that, and was stunned to see there was neither squad car nor NEWOP anywhere to be seen.

"Thank you, dear Lord," Wilbur exclaimed. He knew then that God miraculously had protected him and his family. He no longer had to be convinced of the fact that God had a plan that He wouldn't allow anybody to interfere with.

There was a glimmer of light in the East as the suburban crossed the border into Colorado. "We made it," Wilbur announced triumphantly. Adeline stirred awake in the front seat and looked around with an enormous smile. "He did it," she squealed with delight. "The Lord has proven Himself faithful once again."

Wilbur pulled out a pad of paper to read the directions Paul had given him. There was an old abandoned farm not far away where the family could stay safely away from intruding eyes. When they arrived to the place that had been marked on the map, they spotted an old abandoned barn that was standing in a field which was now overgrown with weeds. Several yards away stood a rundown house that looked like it was about to collapse.

When the car pulled to a stop in front of the barn, the family exited the vehicle and entered the barn. It looked safe enough so they decided they would spend the day there before continuing on that night. In the meantime they would enjoy a meal from a sack with some food that Wilbur retrieved from the back of the suburban. After that they would get some sleep so as to be fresh for the journey still lying ahead. Before settling down though they spent some time in prayer, thanking God for sparing them after their close call. They also thanked him for their food and the good days ahead, knowing that the Lord was always with them.

Chapter Eleven

Johnny Fast Horse

When nightfall came, the family began gathering up everything to pack into the back of the suburban. Off and on between naps, they had spent the day praying and reminiscing about everything they had left behind. Theodora wondered what was going to happen to Heather and her family. Would they make it to safety before the NEWOPS closed in on them? She prayed and lifted them up to the Lord. After that she knew she had to trust Him to protect them. It was all she could do.

Adeline took a comb from her purse and began untangling the long strands of hair before pinning it back up in a bun again. As they began their journey again, she entertained the others with some stories from her childhood.

"Was it really like that, Grandma?" Theodora's eyes were wide with amazement. She was surprised to learn that there had been a time when people could actually vote for the President and Congress. Theodora had never heard that America once had a Senate and House of Representatives. She couldn't imagine what it was like before the New World Government had been set up.

"Grandma, explain it to me. What was voting and how did people do it?" Theodora inquired, her ears pricked up to hear the answer.

"The United States had a government that consisted of three branches – Executive, Legislature, and Judiciary," Adeline began. "The Executive branch consisted of the President and Vice-President. Within this branch was a Cabinet and an advisory board. The President selected who he wanted to serve on his cabinet but the Senate had to approve it. The Vice President automatically served on the Cabinet and it consisted of several departments all of which had separate responsibilities in running the country. The legislature was made up of two houses – The Senate and the House of Representatives. The Judiciary included the Supreme Court and federal courts that were situated throughout the districts in the nation. People chose the President and their members in the House and Senate by casting ballots. That was called voting."

Adeline paused when she saw that she had totally lost Theodora in her efforts to explain the way it used to be. "I know this is hard for you to understand right now, honey. I will wait and tell you more when you get a little older." The child shook her head as she tried to take in what she had been told but it was just too confusing for an 8-year-old. She couldn't fathom the nation ever being like that but she trusted her grandmother and let her mind rest on it for now.

Adeline continued to share more stories that were easier for an 8-year-old to relate to. "I used to help my mother bake cookies to take to the needy. Even though we were poor, things hadn't gotten so bad back then. We still were able to have our own church services in our homes. We didn't suffer as many purges back then," Adeline sighed as she let her mind drift into yesteryears.

The car turned off on to a windy dirt road and there was still quite a trek ahead of them. As they came into the Rocky Mountains it was a treacherous drive through passes with no guard rails. Adeline covered her eyes to hide the view of the sharp cliffs lying dangerously close to her side of the road as the automobile crawled along. Though it was dark the lights from the vehicle revealed steep ravines and overhangs. Theodora, however, found it entertaining. She had never seen mountains before and she thought of this part of the trip as a game. "Faster! Faster!" she cried out in glee to Uncle Wilbur.

"O hush, child," Adeline protested, still burying her eyes in her hands.

As they drove through the mountains and entered a forest they became surrounded on both sides of the road with hundreds of lodge pole pines. Theodora never saw so many trees all in one place and they seemed to reach the heavens. "Wow!" she exclaimed gasping with wonder.

"We are here," Wilbur proclaimed as the vehicle pulled up to a large log building. It was now 6:00 AM and there was smoke climbing out of the chimney announcing that somebody was stirring about inside.

Wilbur was the first to leave the car and was soon knocking at the door of the rustic structure. The others scrabbled out of the suburban and followed behind. Soon the door to the cabin opened and there stood a tall dark complected man in about his mid-fifties. He wore boots and a cowboy hat which were accompanied by a pair of old jeans and a flannel shirt. His hair was long with a braid that reached half-way down his back. It was the first time that Wilbur had set his eyes on Johnny Fast Horse. "Come in! Come in!" he invited with a grin.

The family sat down to a good breakfast, the first hot meal they had had in two days. The food consisted of flat bread made from corn along with some stew cooked with squash, beans, and venison. They would soon learn that this was typical Cherokee cuisine and that they had better get used to it. This would be their sustenance in the days and weeks ahead. Corn, squash and beans along with wild game was the main staple of this tribal group. The White family got to sample some pemmican too. It was made from dried meat and fruit and was used primarily as a survival food for the Indians.

Everyone was soon settled into the bedrooms that would serve them for the night. During their stay, Johnny shared with them some of the history of his people. His ancestors had been driven from their lands east of the Mississippi River during the time of President Andrew Jackson. It was an arduous journey that came to be known as the Trail of Tears. They finally settled in Oklahoma and some of them eventually wound up in Colorado.

Theodora listened intently as Johnny shared story after story. She was especially interested to learn about the revival that broke out on the Indian Reservations during the 21st century. It spread like a wild fire across the plains from state to state. Sweat lodges were transformed into churches. People of the differing tribes soon traded in their drugs, liquor and peyote for Bibles. The chiefs often led worship services. Many of them even became pastors.

After the New World Order was set up, the land on all the reservations were totally turned over to the Indians. Unbeknownst to them, this had all been a part of God's plan. The Native Americans, under the influence of the Holy Spirit, began moving deep into the forests primarily along the mountain ranges. There they set up villages, hundreds of them, and began living the way they had hundreds and thousands of years ago. Theodora noticed that there were horses in a coral but no automobile outside Johnny's cabin. A feeling of excitement grew within her as she anticipated the adventure she would soon embark upon.

Adeline observed Johnny sipping on a cup of coffee as he sat comfortably in a rocking chair, legs crossed.

"You said the Indians live the way they used to," she remarked. "I didn't know they lived in log cabins. I thought they lived in teepees. Besides where did you get the coffee?"

"We have adopted many of the white man's ways and outside of our villages we still enjoy them. However we try to

51

stick to our traditions inside them," Johnny explained. "We have driven automobiles as well in the past but in order to stay away from the suspicious eyes of the NWO we have replaced them with horses even outside the villages."

"Are we going to live with you here forever?" Theodora asked.

"In a few more days I will share more with you," Johnny responded. "For now you will stay right here with me but don't worry. It won't be forever."

"But I like you," Theodora commented. "I wouldn't mind living here with you forever." She smiled big at Johnny. Then she changed the subject. "Can I go play in the woods after lunch?" The sun was now high in the sky indicating the noon meal was at hand.

"You mustn't venture into the woods by yourself," Johnny warned Theodora. "None of you should. It is easy to get lost if you don't know how to traverse this area. I will be happy to teach you all the tricks." Johnny was an expert tracker as well as trapper and hunter. He knew all the tricks of the trade just as all the Indians around there did. They learned from the time they could walk when their fathers would take them into the forest to begin teaching them all about nature. "After lunch I will take you for a walk if you like," he continued.

"Before we sit down to eat you better get your automobile out of sight," Johnny said to Uncle Wilbur. "You won't need it any more, at least not for a long time to come." Wilbur followed him outside and got into the suburban with the big Cherokee sitting in the seat opposite.

Johnny directed him along a pock marked dirt road several hundred feet away until he motioned Wilbur to come to a stop. Then he jumped out of the vehicle and walked up to a steep hill which was covered in vines. He lifted the vines to reveal an opening. When he moved them out of the way there stood a huge cave entrance, leading into a place that was large enough to hide an automobile. Wilbur drove inside and then stepped out of the car. He was surprised to see a jeep parked in there as well as an old buckboard wagon. When he arrived back outside, Johnny moved the vines back into place and the pair walked back towards the cabin.

"What do you use the wagon for?" Wilbur asked scratching his head.

"You will soon see," Johnny answered. The stones along the path scrunched under their feet as they walked along.

"I was surprised to see a jeep too," Wilbur remarked. "I thought you didn't use modern vehicles here."

"The jeep is for emergencies," Johnny explained.

The next morning, Theodora's curiosity got the best of her. She forgot what Johnny had warned her about the night before so she slipped on a light jacket and out the door to do some exploring.

Theodora carried a small pail in her hand which was one she had found in the kitchen of the way station. She was determined to find some berries as a surprise for supper that night. She also had in mind to give Johnny some so she could watch him make pemmican.

As the girl got deeper into the woods, she forgot where she was. After she found some wild berry bushes, she picked all she could find and then turned around to start back. The path didn't look the same and the trees all looked different. Panic began to rise in her as she went this way and that desperately trying to find the path that she had come on. About a half hour went by when she bumped straight into Johnny. She was so relieved that she couldn't say a word.

There was silence all the way back to the cabin as Johnny led the way. Theodora just knew that she was in for a good spanking and she hung her head down once they were back inside. Adeline grabbed her with a big hug and then stood back, a frown on her face.

"What do you mean scaring us so?" Adeline scolded.

"I-I'm sorry," was all Theodora could murmur.

"I have a mind to give you a good licking," Adeline continued.

"Oh don't be so hard on her. I think she learned her lesson already," Johnny cut in, half smiling. "She really had a good scare."

Chapter Twelve

Chota

The White family stayed for two weeks with Johnny Fast Horse while he introduced them to all the habits of the Cherokee tribe. He also prepared them for what they would be exposed to when they reached the village of Chota where he lived. They learned that they weren't the first people who had stayed at the cabin. It served as a rest stop for the Christian refugees who were fleeing persecution. Here they would spend a two week period of indoctrination learning all they needed to know before going on to Chota.

"This isn't the only way station and my village isn't the only one around," Johnny remarked. "There are many, many hundreds of villages scattered throughout the mountains and forests all over the nation. These are countless places of refuge where believers are safely hidden away from the NWO's prying eyes. Tomorrow I will take you to Chota. That is where I live. This place is just my home away from home when I am getting new people ready for the Cherokee way of life. We will leave very early in the morning so be packed and ready to go. It is a long trip by wagon so it will be an all day journey from here."

Theodora listened with excitement. What would the people be like? How would they be dressed? Did the children play games and if so, what kind of games did they enjoy? She smiled in anticipation as she tried to imagine what it would be like.

Johnny told the family how Chota got its name. It had been named after an ancient Cherokee village of refuge that had been excavated in Tennessee. Chota was prominent during the mid 1700's and served as a capital of the Cherokees. It was here where a number of tribal leaders were born and raised. "Today Chota, TN remains an important historical site," Johnny explained. "Every village is named after something that has great meaning for the Indians."

After a supper of flat bread and venison stew, Theodora was tucked into bed where she soon fell into a dream about the Cherokees. The adults stayed up for a while to make final plans for the trip in the morning but they soon retired for the night.

A faint glimmer of the September dawn began displacing the darkness of the night and the stars started to disappear. Johnny had been up for two hours already getting the wagon and horses ready. He had baked the flat bread that he would take for everyone to eat along the way. He also included a sack of pemmican to munch on during the long trek.

Shortly after Johnny had risen, Wilbur and Edna stepped lazily out of bed to get dressed. Theodora was still fast asleep so they didn't want to wake her until it was almost time to leave. Wilbur gaped widely in a yawn as he stretched and then entered the kitchen where Johnny greeted him with a smile. "What's for breakfast?" he inquired.

"Breakfast is going with us," Johnny informed Wilbur. He was busy wrapping up the flat bread and pemmican to take along the journey. The pleasant odor of the freshly baked bread filled the atmosphere in the room and Wilbur deeply breathed it in with a grateful sigh.

Everyone was jostled about as the wagon bumped along on the rough road. Adeline was happy they didn't have to ride horse back at least. She knew her old bones couldn't take it. She tried to imagine what it was like for the people traveling by covered wagons that moved Westward during the gold rush years. "Thank Heavens we only have to travel like this for one day," she sighed. The two horses pulling the wagon were typical

Indian ponies. One was a pinto while the other was a paint. The animals stepped gingerly over the rocks in the road and the trip seemed endless.

"When will we get there?" Theodora inquired restlessly.

"We will get there when we get there," Uncle Wilbur answered.

"It should be shortly after sunset," Johnny said.

Adeline winced, wondering if she would make it until then. She felt every bone in her body was ache already and it wasn't even noon.

Every hour or two Johnny would stop the wagon and share a little flat bread and pemmican with everybody. It was also a chance for people to relieve themselves in the woods. The men would go in one direction and the women in another in order to preserve some privacy. Once back in the wagon the arduous journey would continue.

In order to keep everybody's mind off the rough ride, Johnny told a few Indian stories. He also instructed everyone about the animals and birds that lived in the area. "You need to be careful of rattlesnakes too," he warned.

"Let me tell you about the lodge pole pine," Johnny continued with a smile. "Did you know that the only way this tree can multiply is if it is burned? The heat from the fire opens up the pine cone allowing it to grow into another tree. We Cherokees have continued the practice of controlled burns in the forests in order to rid them of old dead trees and allow for other kinds of firs and pines to take root. Because of the tremendous height of the lodge pole, other evergreens can't grow unless the taller trees are cleared out from time to time."

"Look!" Theodora pointed to something in a tree.

"It's an owl, a great horned owl," Johnny explained. "They are common all over these parts. Did you know that owls sleep

57

during the day? At night they wake up and start hunting for their food."

"I've never seen an owl before," the child remarked. She breathed in the pleasant piney fragrance of the forest. "It smells so good here too."

"Yes!" Edna joined in the conversation. "I've never smelled air as fresh as this."

"This land hasn't been spoiled by city smog and odors," Johnny responded. "I hope it never will be."

Everyone continued to chatter about this or that in order to keep their minds off the continual jostling of the wagon. Time went by faster too. There was one more stop to rest the horses and to allow everyone to enjoy their final meal of the day. Johnny surprised them when he brought out a separate bag of food.

"What is it?" everybody asked in unison.

"This is Cherokee grape bread," Johnny answered. "It is made from wild grapes and is a favorite dessert of mine."

Theodora's mouth watered as she bit into the savory bread. She heard grunts of pleasure as everyone indulged in the unusual dessert. She learned that this was only unusual for her and not for the Native Americans.

The sun had set and the stars were beginning to come out when the wagon finally joggled its way into Chota. Several children bustled up to the wagon and some of them jumped on. Johnny gave each of them a friendly pat and then jumped down to unhitch the horses.

Johnny showed the White family to their log cabin. It was rustic but comfortable. A wood stove stood at one side of the room and there was a fireplace with wood piled high in it. Johnny started it for them so the cabin would remain comfortably warm for the night. Late September nights could be quite chilly even though the village lay in a valley.

It seemed like morning came all too soon. Theodora, however, was excited to run outside to take in the view of her new surroundings. Once outdoors, she looked around to see snow capped peaks of the Rocky Mountains looming high in the distance. She noticed there were many lodges made from river cane and plaster with thatched roofs. These Cherokee homes were interspersed with log cabins throughout the village. The dwellings spread out as far as the eye could see. In the center of the village were three large lodges. Theodora would soon find out that one of them served as a school. The second one served as a church and the third as a tribal council meeting place for the men. The chief resided over the council and he served a population of 2,000 people in the village.

Since it was still very early in the morning, Theodora discovered she was alone with the exception of some young boys at play. She noticed they were dressed in typical Cherokee costume. It was as if she had stepped into the 18th century. The Indians here practiced their dress and customs from centuries ago with some exceptions. They had been introduced to chickens so they learned how to raise them. They also learned how to raise hogs and pigs so they were able to add bacon and sausage to their menu along with the eggs.

Although the chief wanted to stay strictly with the original customs of his tribe, he reluctantly relented and allowed the people to enjoy the bacon and eggs for breakfast they had so happily grown accustomed to. Of course this also allowed for the raising of chickens and pigs but they were never allowed within the perimeters of the village. The clearing in the forest was enormous so it allowed the people enough space to use some of it as farm land for raising some crops. This was located in a far section of the village. Cherokees were excellent farmers and they raised corn, beans, and squash along with some sunflowers. Their diet was supplemented with pemmican to tide them through the winter months.

Johnny was up by now along with the other adults. Edna and Adeline were busy in the kitchen preparing breakfast. After nearly a constant diet of pemmican, flat bread and venison for the last several days the eggs and bacon frying in a pan on the stove looked like a feast. The fragrance drew Theodora into the house and soon the family was enjoying the succulent meal. The flat corn bread which accompanied the meal didn't seem so bad now.

A knock at the door brought Adeline there to answer it. She welcomed Johnny as he stepped in. Everyone was surprised to see his change in dress. Instead of the cowboy hat and boots, he was now wearing a feather in his hair which still hung in a long braid down his back. On his feet were moccasins and he wore leggings and a typical Indian breech cloth. His face was covered with Indian paint but instead of the traditional tribal tattoo art, his cheeks bore red crosses. On his forehead was painted a white dove, all symbols of the Savior. It was Sunday and everyone was invited to the church service that morning.

Inside the church lodge, the White family quietly took a seat on a bench. Many of the natives sat on the dirt floor while the elderly and refugees sat on the more comfortable benches. All the Indians were dressed just as they had been centuries ago.

Pastor Mark Soaring Eagle stood up in the midst of everyone. He was about sixty years of age but his hair was still solid black with no signs of grey. He stood in front of a semi-circle of blankets and buffalo rugs on which the people sat. The pastor looked around and welcomed everybody with a smile.

After his sermon, the pastor led the congregation in a couple of Cherokee Christian songs. A man next to him played a native hand-made flute. The soothing music was beautiful and as everyone listened they felt drawn closer to God. The songs were written by the Cherokees and had become very popular. When the service was over, the White family was invited to a feast of venison that had been roasting over an open fire all morning. Squash and beans were served along with it. After the meal, Johnny took the family on a tour of the village.

"Many different tribes have villages that are run according to their own customs," Johnny shared. "There are the Sioux, the Cree, the Ute, the Navajo, and countless tribes that live in villages scattered throughout these mountains ranging from New Mexico on up through Montana and beyond. Everywhere you see mountains in this nation you will find villages of refuge."

"How did you come to know Jesus?" Wilbur asked.

"During the time of my ancient ancestors, a missionary came and brought Bibles to our people. Many were saved but as the years went by a spiritual coldness began to rest upon the people. They drifted away from the one true God and began to worship the false gods of the native people," Johnny explained.

"Then several years ago, a revival broke out among the Cherokee. It spread like a wildfire from tribe to tribe all across the nation. This was during the time we still lived on reservations owned by the government. My great grandfather was a boy then. He saw Jesus in a dream one night. After that he was radically saved. He was determined to follow Jesus and eventually was called into the ministry. He was one of the first tribal pastors who had come out of that great revival." Johnny's eyes lit up as he recalled everything his father had related to him about his ancestor.

"Come," Johnny said. "I want you to meet someone."

The family followed Johnny to a lodge and then on inside with him. In the center of the lodge sat an old man. He was sitting Indian style, his head bowed in prayer. When he heard them he looked up and everybody was introduced. The old man turned out to be Johnny's father, chief of the village.

Chapter Thirteen

The Chota Grammar School

Theodora sat in the classroom of her new school. The students sat in a semicircle with the instructor standing before them. Everyone had a deer skin tablet with charcoal pencils with which to write. The teacher wrote on a deer skin which was attached to a board. She was writing down words using the Cherokee alphabet. "Such strange letters," Theodora thought to herself. They were different from the alphabet she had been used to. She learned that this had been invented by George Guess, Chief Sequoyah of the Cherokee. It had been developed between 1809 and 1824. Cherokee is a polysynthetic language with a syllabary writing system.

Theodora was assigned a student tutor by the name of Naomi Rising Moon. She was 12 years old and the two girls were soon best friends. They stayed after school so Naomi could instruct Theodora in the native language. Theodora was bright and soon became prolific in both speaking and writing Cherokee.

The teacher, Connie East Winds, praised her, "You are special, Theodora. I sense that God has chosen you for a special purpose."

Those words sounded familiar; Theodora remembered that day when her father spoke those very same words to her before he was dragged off by the NEWOPS. God would continue to remind her throughout the years that He had a special plan for her life. Theodora thought about it a lot and would often gaze into the distance as she pondered on it.

"Do you think the NEWOPS will bother us here?" Theodora asked Johnny one day.

"We are hidden away where it would be very difficult for any outsider to find us," Johnny responded. "You don't need to fear as long as you follow the rules."

The rules consisted of these:

1. Nobody was to leave the village under any circumstances unless special permission was given and then only with the escort of a tribal member.

2. Everyone was to keep spiritually attuned to God through daily prayer and Bible reading. It was highly recommended that everyone attend the morning and evening devotional times that were held in the church lodge.

3. Everybody was to work together cooperatively. They were to follow Paul's command in 2 Thessalonians 3:10 which said, "For even when we were with you we gave you this rule: 'If a man will not work, he shall not eat.'"

Therefore everyone was assigned chores to do. The women prepared the meals and tanned the hides of the large game which had been brought home from the hunting grounds. They also worked in the fields, some of them with babies strapped in carriers on their backs. The men fished and hunted wild turkeys, deer, and small game to bring home for the cooking pots. The small children had the jobs of gathering sticks and pinecones for building the cooking fires which were situated towards the center of the lodges. The older children were taught survival skills.

There was a strict work ethic among the Cherokees. Everyone had chores to do, each according to his own ability. Nobody was exempt. The elderly were given the easier jobs of basket or bead work. They also helped with the preparation of food. As a result everyone had the complete satisfaction that they were contributing something. There wasn't a lazy person among them.

Everyone was all too happy to contribute what they could and the Christian refugees worked right alongside the Cherokee villagers. They were so thankful to the Indians for rescuing them from the NWO Death Camps. They were being received by the thousands into the various hidden villages of refuge throughout the mountains and forest lands. Although it wasn't required many of them began learning the languages of the Cherokee, Navajo, Ute, Sioux, Crow, and numerous other tribal groups. Difficult as it was to acclimate to their strange environments, they wanted to fit in with their new friends as much as possible. The confinement to the village was the most difficult thing to cope with.

One day Theodora started to complain. "Grandma, how long do we have to be here? I'm beginning to feel like I'm in jail." She went on and on about how hard it was.

Then Adeline broke in and interrupted her angry tirade. "Shame on you," she scolded. "You should get on your knees and thank God for what He has done for us here. He has given us new friends who have literally saved our lives. If it weren't for them we probably would be dead or in some NWO labor camp somewhere. Besides, our lives haven't been so bad here. Sure, it has been a big adjustment but look at all we have learned from these people and especially Johnny Fast Horse."

"I'm sorry, Grandma," Theodora answered with chagrin. Then she got down on her knees to ask God for forgiveness and to help her be more thankful for what she had.

"Do you think God is going to keep us here forever?" Theodora asked wryly.

"No, child," Adeline smiled. "It is all in God's timing and plan."

There it was. God had brought it to Theodora's attention again, reminding her that He had a plan. It was like a common thread running through her life repetitively to constantly remind her that she had been chosen. Perhaps God was trying to encourage her and give her the patience to wait upon Him no matter her circumstances.

When school was dismissed the following day, Theodora and Naomi remained after class. After the tutoring session, the girls busied themselves with cleaning up the cinders from the fire. They also straightened out the desks and seats which had been made from pine logs. Then before leaving they cleaned off the charcoal letters from the deerskin board the teacher had written on that day.

Naomi taught Theodora how to sew beadwork onto women's clothing. This seemed more like play than work to the 8-year-old. She caught on fast and looked forward to the time each day when she could use her creative skills to make up new designs. Theodora grew more content with her new surroundings as the days passed. She rejoiced with the fact that the women were delighted with her creations. Theodora smiled with glee when they would hurry to the market in the village to buy clothing that was newly decorated by her. She noticed that there was no exchange of money though.

"How do people buy things?" Theodora queried.

"We don't use money like those outside the village do?" Naomi answered.
"We use a barter system. When somebody brings in a deer skin, pottery, jewelry or some other item a piece of chalk is used to mark it according to its value. Then the person selling it is given a credit to be used towards something they want to buy. He can purchase something in the market with the credit he has saved up. Do you understand?"

Theodora nodded but her brow was furled with puzzlement. "I guess so."

"You will get used to it in time," Naomi assured.

"I am happy to see so many women selling the clothes with my beadwork on it," Theodora smiled. It wasn't long when she caught on to the Cherokee bartering system.

Theodora loved to go to the market and get some special Cherokee sweets to savor. She had nothing to trade so she would do special chores at the market to earn some credit. She worked hard all day on Saturday so she could purchase the tasty treats to take home for her family to enjoy that very same night.

"Grandma, I'm beginning to like it here," Theodora announced one night as she was being tucked into bed. "In fact I'm starting to have a lot of fun."

"See, honey! When you learn to thank God instead of complaining you start to appreciate the little things He gives you." Adeline heard Theodora's prayers and kissed her goodnight.

Chapter Fourteen

Treasure Trove

It was a Saturday morning when Johnny came knocking at Wilbur's door. "Come in! Come in!" Wilbur greeted. "You are just in time to join us for a little breakfast." "Thank you but I already ate. I will have some coffee though," Johnny answered. He sat down to enjoy a steaming cup of coffee. Then his eyes lit up with a smile. "I want to show you something," Johnny announced. After breakfast Wilbur followed him outside. Presently they came to a hill with a locked door in the side. It was a cave that had been dug out by hand years ago. When Johnny unlocked the door and they entered, Wilbur got the surprise of his life. There were mounds of books stacked everywhere.

"Wh-What is this?" Wilbur exclaimed. When he examined the pile of books more closely he discovered they were among those which had been outlawed by the NWO. These included Dickens, Shakespeare, Keats, and C. S. Lewis as well as numerous other great authors and poets. Wilbur sucked in his breath as he shuffled through them. Then his eyes bulged out with astonishment. He picked up an old black book. On it was printed "Holy Bible." It was a King James Version. "Where did you get this?" Wilbur gasped with excitement.

"We managed to hide this one away before the NEWOPS could grab them all," Johnny said. "It was during the time of the great confiscation and book burning when we built this place with our own hands in order to protect all this written treasure. It is so valuable to us that we don't allow any of these volumes out of this cave."

"Thank you, Johnny! Thank you for all you have done for us." Wilbur gave Johnny a hug of gratitude.

"When we were in Topeka, there were store houses of books hidden away there also," Wilbur continued. "My mother bought or borrowed some of them to read. Her favorite author is C. S. Lewis. Her grandmother cut her teeth on his novels."

"We have been praying for a long time that books like these as well as the Bible will be available to the general public once again," Johnny remarked.

Wilbur and his family marveled at the great intelligence and close walk with God that the Cherokees had. They saw many healings and miracles take place at the prayer services in the church. Johnny's father, Chief White Crane, always was in attendance. Wilbur was amazed because the old chief was 90 years old and yet in perfect health, his hearing and vision that of a youngster. "What keeps everybody in such good health?" Wilbur asked.

"It is a combination of our diet and faith. We also get plenty of exercise and outdoor activity," Johnny shared. "The air is pure around here, as well, so we aren't breathing in all the smoke and chemicals of the cities."

This was true among the other tribes too. Since the revival had broken out there was no alcohol or drugs among the Indians. The sweat lodges were replaced by churches everywhere. Medicine men were replaced by doctors. Many more herbs were discovered which were used for cures to diseases that hadn't yet been discovered in the outside world – cures for Alzheimer's and cancer – cures for diabetes, Parkinson's and even multiple sclerosis.

The Cherokees had discovered many preventative natural drugs as well. They learned how to prevent Down's syndrome by giving women a special herb they had discovered growing in the forest. It was given to girls when they reached puberty which prevented them from ever giving birth to a child with that disorder. Wilbur shook his head in amazement as he took in all this information. How did the Indians learn all these things that the best doctors and scientists in the outside world had no answers for? Could it be supernatural wisdom only God could give?

"In time I will show you something else," Johnny said. "When the time is right and Theodora is ready I will show it to both of you."

Wilbur scratched his head. "What is it?"

"You will find out in God's timing. Just remember that Theodora will have a large part to play in His plan," Johnny answered.

Wilbur thought back, in his mind, to the time God had spoken to his brother about the plan. Nobody ever knew what it was nor did they understand it. Yet God kept reminding him of it. As much as he wanted to know every detail of it, he knew he would have to wait. God never revealed anything before the time was ripe to carry it out.

Wilbur picked up a book by Shakespeare. "Can I take this back home to read?"

"Nothing must leave this cave," Johnny warned. "Although people around here seem to be trustworthy, we can't ever be sure that there isn't a spy among us. This place is as secure as we could make it but we never can be sure if the NEWOPS have detected us and sent somebody in to spy on us."

"What could be done if that were to happen?" Wilbur asked, alarm in his voice.

"We do have a place, hidden away, where very few of us know about," Johnny answered. "We haven't had to use it yet. We hope we never have to - but if we are forced to, we can take everybody there. I don't think the NEWOPS will ever be able to find that place. We have given it a name – Painted Cavern."

Wilbur felt a sense of relief as the pair walked back to his cabin. The sun had arisen high in the sky by now. He couldn't believe how fast the morning had raced by.

"You must stay and have lunch with us," Wilbur invited. "No excuses this time," he smiled. Johnny consented. He lived alone because he was single and had no family other than his spiritual one. Johnny was to enjoy many meals with the White family from that day on as they continued to learn from one another.

Chapter Fifteen

Lost

To get ready for the winter, several men from the village traveled north to hunt buffalo. Their hides would be used not only for food but for warm clothing. They would also cover the doorways to the lodges which would provide extra warmth against the wind and snow. There was no waste. Every part of the body would serve some useful purpose.

Winter seemed endless causing Theodora to feel more penned up than ever. "When will spring come?" she asked her grandmother, impatience in her voice.

"It will be here soon enough," Adeline assured. "In the meantime there are plenty of things to keep us busy."

Indeed there was. Theodora continued to learn the difficult Cherokee language and she practiced it regularly with Naomi and other people she came into contact with on a regular basis. She also continued sewing beads on lady's clothing. Her designs became more original and decorative as the weeks and months went by. She found much pleasure in doing these things. Yet she longed for a change.

Finally spring came and the forthcoming change along with it. Theodora was soon to embark on a new journey.

It was evening and Tommy Screaming Eagle had just returned from the forest with some small game he had trapped. After trading some of his furs at the market, he set in to make a few new traps. Theodora was walking by and became interested in what the boy was doing. "He seems rather young to be doing this," she thought to herself.

"How old are you?" Theodora inquired in her halting Cherokee language.

"I'm twelve years old. How old are you?" Tommy answered. Theodora was able to understand him much better than speak in his language.

"I will be nine years old next month." Theodora's expression was inquisitive. "By the way, what is your name?"

"Tommy," the boy answered. "What's yours?"

"Theodora," the girl replied, looking intently at what Tommy was doing. "What is all that?"

"My traps! I'm getting ready to go trapping in the morning," the boy responded.

"Aren't you kind of young to be doing that sort of thing?" Theodora asked.

"O no! I started learning how to trap when I was five years old. My father took me with him whenever he went. As you can see we make our own traps." It was a simple one made especially for small game.

"I see! What animals do you trap?" Theodora asked, wrinkling her nose.

"Mostly hares and foxes." Tommy never looked up from his work. "Elk, deer, and bear are hunted with bows and arrows. We go hunting for the big game late every fall and can be gone as long as a week. We always go in groups then. It provides more safety for us against cougar and bear attacks. Last year when we went hunting for the buffalo we were gone for a lot longer."

"That sounds like fun," Theodora commented. "Can I go with you in the morning?"

"Girls don't trap or hunt," Tommy snorted. "That is just for the men."

"All I want to do is watch. Besides I'm tired of being stuck in this village all the time. I need a change," Theodora pouted.

"If the chief gives permission, you can come," Tommy relented. He went and spoke to his father who then went in to

73

see the chief. Theodora stood anxiously waiting outside the chief's lodge. When Tommy's father returned, he had a smile on his face for Theodora. "You can go," he said with a twinkle in his eye. "Just remember. All you are permitted to do is just watch. You aren't allowed to touch the traps or the game." A stern look replaced the smile on the man's face. Theodora had a difficult time understanding all the Indian ways. "Why can't girls hunt and trap just like men?" she grumbled to herself. Yet she was thankful she was allowed to go at all.

Theodora let out a squeal of delight and ran home to tell her family about the adventure she was about to embark upon. That night she was too excited to sleep much. She kept waking up to see if the eastern horizon was starting to light up. When it finally did, it was the sign for her to get ready to leave. She grabbed the parcel of breakfast that had been left on the table the night before. Aunt Edna packed enough for both Theodora and Tommy.

Theodora waited outside Tommy's lodge and it wasn't long before he made his appearance. Rolled up in a bear skin were several small traps he had made. He had them tucked under his arm. Soon the two were off towards the woods. Tommy marked the trees along the way as Theodora gleefully followed. For several hundred yards they trudged along a well worn path before veering off to go deeper into the forest. Tommy continued to mark the trees with a piece of white chalk. "Why are you doing that?" Theodora finally asked.

"This is so we won't get lost," Tommy answered. "The marks on the trees will tell us where we have been. I also watch carefully where the grass has been trampled down underneath our feet. All these telltale signs show where we have gone and how to get back." Theodora marveled at how smart the young boy was. She hoped to learn all these Indian tricks herself so she could take a walk in the woods by herself one day.

Soon they arrived at a spot where Tommy set a trap. Several yards later he set another one. He continued until about two dozen had been set. Then they made their way westward for about a mile. By now the sun was high in the sky. Theodora opened the packet of food her aunt had prepared. She and Tommy had already eaten part of the meal of pemmican and Cherokee tortillas. Now their hungry stomachs begged for the remainder.

After their brief respite, they continued on until they came to some more traps that Tommy had set the day before. Some of the traps contained rabbits and foxes while others hadn't yet been sprung. Tommy gathered up the small game and announced that it was time to start back. "It is at least two miles back to the village," he said. "We need to get back there before dark sets in." Theodora nodded her head vigorously in agreement, unaware of what waited just ahead of them.

The pair had just started back when a furry brown giant rose up in front of them. It was a male grizzly bear. Theodora screamed and jumped away. There was loud yelling and rustling. Theodora screamed some more and ran. When she looked back she saw the bear tossing Tommy around on the ground with its long, sharp claws.

Theodora ran and ran until she could run no more. Her chest heaved in and out as she sucked oxygen into her lungs. When she finally caught her breath she looked around in terror with the realization that she was lost. She had no idea how to get back. She didn't know any of the Indian tricks when it came to traversing through the forest. Not being able to find her way out of the forest wasn't the only thing that frightened her. It was the thought of not knowing where that bear was. She began to move as fast as she could again, all the time glancing behind her to see if it was closing in on her.

As she continued running Theodora came to a clearing. She noticed a hill with an opening in it. As it beckoned to her, she scrambled towards it. The opening was so small she could barely squeeze through it. At least the bear wouldn't be able to come in after her. When she was safely inside she let out a long breath of relief. "Thank you, Jesus!" she prayed silently. Then fear swept over her again. How would she find her way home? And who could ever find her way out here? What about Tommy? Was he dead? Would they find him? Would he be ok? Tears streamed down her face as she thought about all these things.

Theodora felt like hours had gone by as she lay there helpless in the tiny cave. She noticed that the light outside was dimming which meant that it was getting dangerously late. But she didn't dare leave. What if the bear was close by? Soon there were indications that it was. She could hear a snuffling outside the cave.

In terror, she moved back inside the cave as far as she could go. She heard some more commotion just outside so she held her breath and shut her eyes tightly while pursing her lips. She cried out to the Lord, "Jesus, please save me. Please...please...please!" Soon it became quiet outside and she fell into a fitful sleep. She dreamed about the bear chasing after her. She could scarcely move her feet and legs as the beast drew closer and closer. She tried to scream but couldn't make a sound. Then a voice called her name. It called again and again. Theodora woke up with a start. Then she realized she had heard the voice when she was asleep.

"Theodora, where are you?" the voice cried again.

Quickly Theodora crawled out of the cave and yelled, "Johnny, is that you?" She had recognized his voice in the dark. She looked around and saw a figure carrying a torch.

Theodora, where are you?" Johnny cried.

"I'm here," she answered. "I'm right over here."

"O, thank God! Are you all right?"

"Yes, Johnny! I am fine now." Theodora's expression of delight suddenly turned to deep concern. "What about Tommy? Did you find him?"

"Yes, Theodora," Johnny smiled

"Is he dead?" Theodora had an expression of deep concern on her face.

"No, Theodora. Tommy is fine. He suffered a few deep scratches from the bear's claws but he will be just fine. He is back at the village getting treated now. In a few days he will be as good as new." Johnny gave Theodora a look of assurance.

"Oh I'm so glad. I thought that bear killed him."

"Tommy has been taught what to do in the event of a bear attack. He laid face down on the ground and curled up into a fetal position with his hands around the back of his neck. That way the bear thought he was dead and left after he had tossed him around for a bit. You never want to run away from a bear that is attacking you. He is much faster than you are."

After Johnny returned Theodora safely home with her family, they all thanked him profusely and invited him in for a late supper. Nobody had eaten yet. Nobody had been hungry, not knowing where Theodora was. Now everyone was ready to sit down and enjoy the evening meal. They all joined hands along with Johnny and gave thanks to God for Theodora's life.

Chapter Sixteen

Cheyenne Justice

Willie Whistling Winds was holding an iPhone in his hand when two braves, part of the tribal police force, burst into his lodge. They had revolvers and they were pointing them right at Willie's head. "You are under arrest. Come with us," one of them yelled.

In shock and shaking, Willie put his iPhone down and began following them. One of the Cheyenne braves picked up the iPhone to take along with them. Soon the three entered the tribal council lodge. Chief White Crane, donned in his head dress and buffalo robe, was seated in the center. He wore a stern expression.

"Here is the evidence," Joe Fox Who Runs, one of the braves told the chief; he handed the iPhone to him.

The Cherokees had patterned their legal system after the U.S. judiciary. They had a court, a judge, lawyers, and a jury. Their chief always served as the judge. They also had a militia to protect the village. Since the Cherokee nation had made a declaration of war with the NWO any act that put the village in jeopardy was considered treason.

Willie had been caught with an iPhone and this was against tribal law. After examining the device it was discovered that Willie had sent emails back and forth to some NEWOP leaders. There was evidence that proved Willie's guilt. He had collaborated with them in a plan to attack Chota and take it over.

Willie had been one of the faithful servants in the church for many years so it came as a shock when this was discovered. In the beginning Willie was happy and content but as time went on he became jealous over those in leadership. He desired a position

78

of more authority and when his requests for such were denied, he grew bitter and angry. The hatred grew inside until he started plotting revenge against those he thought were holding him back.

One day he discovered an iPhone that had been left in a counseling room of the church. The pastor apparently had forgotten it. Most of the people were forbidden to have iPhones for fear they could cause mischief and take their attention away from God. Only the pastor, the chief and certain members of the militia and Underground were allowed to have them.

The trial lasted several weeks and Willie had a defense lawyer who argued his case. The prosecution brought forth very convincing evidence of Willie's guilt, however. When the jury brought in the final verdict he was pronounced guilty.

"Do you know what this means?" Chief White Crane asked grimly.

Willie hung his head and nodded. He fully understood the consequences of his guilt.

The Cheyenne nation had adopted the same penalty that was used in the white man's military during times of war. Acts of treason were punished by execution before a firing squad. Since they were living in a state of war Willie was about to face the same fate. He was led back to his holding cell that had been built in the side of one of the hills.

When Theodora heard about it she felt sad. "Why does he have to die?" she asked Johnny Fast Horse one morning.

"We have laws and some of them are very important. The reason they are so strict is because we have to protect everyone in the village. We are at war with the NWO. This is why we have a militia," Johnny answered. "If we didn't have consequences for breaking the law, people would continue to break it. Some crimes aren't as serious as others so the penalties are lighter. We regard treason as very serious. Treason is when a person betrays his own people and puts them in grave jeopardy. What Willie did was an act of treason. He betrayed us to the NEWOPS. Now in order to give extra protection to the village, we have been forced to put extra guards at the gates of entry to the village. We may even have to evacuate everyone from here and hide them in Painted Cavern."

At this Theodora felt alarm well up inside her. "Willie is a very evil man," she said with anger.

"What Willie did was evil but we must remember that God loves him," Johnny reminded her. "Willie must die for what he did but we must pray for him. He has strayed away from God but it isn't too late for him to come back. We don't want him to wind up in Hell and neither does God. Tonight we are all going to pray for Willie at our prayer meeting. I hope you will find it in your heart to pray for him too."

That night everybody was on their knees with heartfelt prayers for Willie. Many tears were shed as their requests were lifted up to Heaven. Theodora felt her heart soften towards Willie as she prayed. She understood that she was just as guilty before God if she didn't have Jesus. "We are all capable of sin. We can all be deceived," the pastor reminded everyone. "When our brother falls we need to lift him up. But for the grace of God, there go we. We must always remember this."

Pastor Soaring Eagle visited Willie daily and admonished him to turn his heart back to God.

"It's too late for me," Willie argued.

"No! You are wrong. It's never too late. Remember the thief on the cross. He admitted to Jesus that he was a sinner. Then he gave his heart to Him right then and there," the pastor shared. "Do you remember what Jesus told him?"

"No," Willie admitted. "I don't."

"Jesus said, 'Today you shall be with me in Paradise.'" A tear slid down the pastor's face as he looked at Willie, compassion in his eyes.

Willie bent his head down and began to sob. He didn't see how God could love somebody like him. After a few minutes he looked up at the pastor and said, "Can He love me so much as to forgive me for what I did?"

"Peter denied Jesus three times. Later on he became a great evangelist and he brought many, many souls to Christ. If God could forgive Peter for turning his back on Jesus not once but three times, don't you think He can forgive you?" The pastor smiled warmly. Willie nodded.

"Will you pray with me?" Willie wept. "I want God back in my life."

"Yes, Willie," the pastor replied with a sniffle. The pair of men knelt down and prayed for about a half hour. Every last bit of guilt and remorse was cleansed from Willie's heart and conscience. When they had spoken their last, Willie was beaming. He was a brand new person and ready to meet the Lord the next morning.

That night five of the militia men were glumly cleaning their rifles. They dreaded what they would have to do in the morning.

Pastor Soaring Eagle entered the lodge where the men were busily preparing for their grim task.

"You don't need to look so sad," the pastor remarked. The men looked up, their brows furled in surprise.

"Everything is going to be fine," the pastor continued.

"You mean the execution is off?" one of the men asked.

"No! I'm afraid the execution has to take place. What I meant is the prisoner is now ready to meet God!" the pastor smiled.

"I don't understand. How can that be?" came the reply.

"He has surrendered his life to Jesus. He is looking forward to being with Him forever." The pastor beamed with the good news and the men all smiled with relief.

The sun began peeking over the hills and the firing squad stood ready, five men with their rifles standing at attention awaiting their final orders. Willie was brought out by one of the tribal council members.

"Do you want a blindfold?" he asked Willie.

"No!" Willie answered. "I will be just fine." His face was lit up with a supernatural joy and peace that only God could give as he waited to appear before the Bema Seat of Christ. He anticipated what Jesus would say. "I don't remember your sins, my child. Enter into my House where I have prepared a place for you."

When the final order was given, Willie wasn't even aware of what just took place. As he bowed his head in death, he saw two angels appear before him. They each took one of his hands and gently lifted him up into glory.

"Death has been swallowed up in victory. Where, O death is your victory? Where, O death, is your sting?" the angels sang and Willie joined in with them.

Chapter Seventeen

Forbidden Ride

Theodora had it all planned out. She would sneak out of the prayer meeting early when nobody would notice. When she entered the lodge she would deliberately sit next to the door where it would be easy to slip out from under watching eyes. Her horse would be her taxi out of there.

Several years had passed and Theodora was now fourteen years old. She had grown tall like her birth father had been, reaching nearly 5'11". She remembered that day on her ninth birthday when Johnny Fast Horse gave her that mare. She had named her Annabelle and would ride her every day. She wasn't allowed to leave the village except to go into the forest and then she had to have a companion along with her. As the years passed, however, Theodora had grown more and more restless and her teenage curiosity about the outside world grew along with it. She had inherited her inquisitiveness from her father, Reverend Hobart Jackson.

Up to now, Theodora had been very obedient and was careful to follow all the rules ever since she and her family came to Chota. Her memory of the world out there and the city she came from had grown dim in her mind. She had been barely eight-years-old when she left Topeka with her family. The memory of Pastor White's face, however, remained clear in her mind. Often she wondered if he might still be alive somewhere. Nobody had ever told her the horrid truth of what had happened to him. After pondering on it, Theodora realized that if he were alive he would have contacted her and the others by now. Nothing could have kept her father away, no NEWOP, not even an earthquake. She swelled with pride as she realized he must have died a hero somewhere.

Evening came and Theodora sat by the door in the church lodge waiting for the opportune time to sneak out. She had tied Annabelle close by in order to make a quick get-away. At last her chance came and she quietly crawled out of the lodge and made her way to the awaiting horse. She climbed on the mare and galloped away.

Wilbur heard the hoof beats of the rapidly retreating horse and wondered who it could be. Not noticing that Theodora was missing, he gave it no more thought and resumed praying. Perhaps it was just one of the sentries making his way to the guard post by the village gate. These guards served in four hour shifts throughout a 24-hour day.

Theodora knew better than to try to go through the closely guarded village gate so she chose a path leading into the forest. It eventually took her out to a dirt road which connected to a paved one leading into the town of Gunnison. The sun was getting low on the summer horizon and Theodora started to think that she had made a grave mistake. "I need to turn right around and go back," she thought to herself. She scolded herself for not thinking things through before planning this trip. She had forgotten about the NEWOPS who might be holed up in Gunnison.

Although the dirt road she was on wasn't well traveled, a NEWOP might decide to surveil it out. As her thoughts grew darker and darker she decided to turn back. She was afraid to go back to Chota though. She shuddered as she thought about what the tribal council might do to her. She had never forgotten what happened to Willy Whistling Winds a few years back. Just as she was ready to turn her horse around she saw a pair of headlights in the distance. She paused and then noticed that they were rapidly closing in on her. Having brought Annabelle to a complete halt she sat on her mount, literally frozen in fear.

The oncoming vehicle came to a stop and a NEWOP stepped out. He was a large man, tall and rough looking with a scowl on his face.

"Get off your horse," he ordered.

Theodora quietly dismounted, not daring to say a word.

"Leave your horse and come with me," the NEWOP demanded. He grabbed the girl by the arm and half drug her to the waiting police car.

"Get in!" the man barked. The fifty mile drive to Gunnison seemed to take forever as Theodora sat in the back seat, trying to muffle her terrified sobs.

Back at the village, everyone noticed by now that Theodora had disappeared. The men began frantically searching while the women stayed back to pray. Wilbur asked the guards at the gate if they had seen her but nobody had noticed her leaving. Every nook and cranny of the village was searched.

"This is my entire fault," Wilbur sighed. "If I had investigated when I heard the horse galloping away, this wouldn't have happened." He shook his head and hung it down in remorse.

Pastor Soaring Eagle put his hand compassionately on Wilbur's shoulder and spoke softly to him. "Nobody is at fault. This is a time to pray instead of casting blame."

After searching everywhere, everybody returned to the church lodge and resumed prayer, this time for a miracle.

The NEWOP vehicle finally pulled into a police station in Gunnison. By this time the NWO had control over every police station in every town and city in the United States. The burly man stepped out of the car, opened the door on Theodora's side, grabbed her roughly by the arm and jerked her out.

Inside the station Theodora was introduced to a matron who was dressed in the same beige uniform that the policemen (NEWOPS) wore. However her uniform consisted of a skirt and nylons instead of trousers. Her outfit was identical to that of the men otherwise. She wore a white shirt and black tie underneath her jacket. Instead of jackboots she wore a pair of black shoes and on her head a beige beret that matched her uniform. The expression on her face was threatening, sending a chill through Theodora.

"Where are you from?" the matron spoke gruffly. "You ain't from around here." Theodora remained silent but her lower lip was trembling.

"You are going to tell me," the matron bellowed. Her name was Madeline Winters and her figure was as foreboding as her voice. Theodora figured she must weigh at least 250 pounds and was around 5'10" in height. If it wasn't for her full figured bosom, Theodora could have easily mistaken her for a man.

Madeline took Theodora into another room. It was painted grey from the ceiling to the walls, and even the floor. There were bars on the windows and the room was empty except for a pole in the center; it had a hitch attached to it. The sight of it terrified Theodora.

"I will give you ten seconds to tell me who you are and where you come from," Madeline warned. Tears ran down Theodora's frightened face but her mouth was clenched tightly shut.

"Guard!" Madeline shouted. A bear of a man entered the room.

"Tie this girl up to that pole," the matron demanded. The man took the girl roughly by the hands and after tying them together, he tied the rope to the hitching pole. Theodora was so tightly fastened to it she couldn't move. Her blouse was ripped, baring her back. As she stood there she watched in horror as the man took a rubber hose in his hand.

Theodora closed her eyes tightly as the man brought the hose sharply across her back three or four times. With each strike tears gushed from her eyes and loud yelps of pain flew from her mouth. Her yells could be heard outside by people who were walking by the window but they didn't pay much notice. Passersby had gotten used to the agonizing screams coming from Christians who were being tortured. Their hearts had gotten hardened towards those who were suffering so unjustly; they just ignored them and continued on their way.

"Are you ready to talk now?" Madeline blared, her face scarlet with anger. The big man stood, breathing heavily, with the hose still in his hand. His lips curled in a cruel smile and his eyes appeared to penetrate right through Theodora. The girl looked back at him, her eyes filled with terror, but she had inherited the iron will of her birth father. She refused to talk even after a few more hard strikes of the hose left her back bruised and bloody.

"Guard, take this girl to her cell now," Madeline ordered. "She won't be any use to us if we kill her. Let her think about it for awhile. Then she will be ready to talk."

Theodora soon found herself locked in a small cell, so tiny she could neither stand nor lie down. As she sat there, her head almost touching the ceiling, she cried silently to the Lord. "I'm sorry for disobeying You," she prayed. "Please get me out of here, sweet Jesus." Then she remembered one of the lessons from Sunday school. Paul and Silas had been beaten and put in prison. But instead of complaining they began to sing and praise God. So she began to sing one of her favorite worship songs. She continued to sing and pray for about an hour and the time passed by quickly then. At last she heard a key turning in the door. "Are they going to beat me some more?" A sharp pang of fear shot through her again.

The cell door opened and a large masculine hand grabbed her and pulled her out. After a few moments she realized this man wasn't taking her back to the torture chamber. He was taking her somewhere else; but where? Soon Theodora found herself being shoved into a room with a bed and shocking lewd pictures hanging on the wall. Besides a small table and chair there was no other furniture in the room. Theodora was horrified as she became aware of what was about to happen to her. After the man closed and locked the door behind them, he faced the girl and looked at her, his mouth twisted up in a leer and his eyes full of lust. Theodora tried to escape, darting this way and that about the room but it was useless. Her attacker was too fast and strong and he finally grabbed her.

"Hold still, you black b....," the man panted, "and take what's coming to you." He graphically described what he was going to do to her as a torrent of foul language shot out of his mouth. As he forced her down onto the bed, she could feel his hot breath that reeked of alcohol.

"Jesus, help me," Theodora yelled at the top of her lungs.

"Your Jesus can't help you now," the man jeered as he tore at her clothes.

Just as the unspeakable was about to happen, Theodora heard a stern voice call from behind her. "Let this girl go before I break your skull." Immediately the assailant released her and fled the room as quickly as he could.

Standing before her was a man with a kind face and a gentle smile. The terror Theodora felt was soon replaced by a sense of peace and gratefulness. She wondered if he was an angel whom Jesus had sent to rescue her. Yet he looked like a man and he was dressed like one too. But didn't Paul, in the Bible, speak of angels that appeared as men?

The man gave her a jacket to wear over her ripped blouse and gently took her by the hand. He led her back to the dirt road without saying a word. Theodora looked up at him with gratitude in her eyes and noticed his face had a curious glow about it. When they had walked together for about a mile, the man dropped her hand and spoke softly in a friendly voice. "You are safe now, Theodora. There is someone here to take you home."

How did he know her name? She had never told him. This was evidence that he really was some kind of supernatural being sent by God.

Theodora looked ahead and saw another figure about 100 yards away. Even though it was dark a heavenly glow brightened the road allowing her to see who it was. It was Johnny Fast Horse standing beside his jeep, the one he used in an emergency such as this.

Theodora ran to Johnny who enveloped her in his arms. Tears of relief and joy glided down her cheeks. "Did you see him?" she asked at last.

"No! Were you with someone?" Johnny replied.

Theodora turned around and saw there was no trace of her rescuer. "He was there," she cried. "He was right there." She pointed to where the man had been.

Then the girl looked back at Johnny. "How did you find me?" she wondered.

"We were praying," Johnny said, "when a strange man entered the church and told me where you were. He gave me detailed directions of how to find you. Then he was gone just as suddenly as he had come. That is why I am here."

Theodora realized then that it wasn't just her imagination. God really did send an angel to rescue her.

On the hour ride back home, Theodora asked about her horse. She was relieved to learn that Annabelle had found her way back to the village.

When they arrived home, one of the native women bathed her wounds and then applied a special balm to them. The ointment was made from herbs the Indians had discovered years before which contained a very effective healing substance. It was nearly 2:00 AM and Theodora was exhausted from her ordeal. She thanked God again and again for what He had done for her. Then she drifted off into a sound sleep. She didn't know then what she would be facing in the morning.

When the sun crawled up into the sky and breakfast was over, Theodora was called to appear before the tribal council. Her heart raced with fear of what punishment would be meted out to her. She shuddered in horror as her wild imagination caused her to envision herself standing before a firing squad. After all she had broken one of their laws and she never remembered any disobedient person escaping the consequences, not since she had come to live in Chota. Now as she stood before the chief trembling, she waited to hear his dire verdict.

Instead of the stern look the chief always wore on his face just before sentencing a law breaker, he smiled. Theodora felt a sense of relief sweep through her body. Maybe he was going to let her off the hook.

"I could punish you for disobeying our rules," the chief said as he drew the buffalo robe more firmly about his shoulders. "I talked it over with the other members of the council and we decided you already suffered the consequences of what you did. Therefore you are being acquitted." Then the chief's face took on a serious expression. "But we don't take law breaking lightly. Next time you won't get off so easily," he warned.

"Does that mean I won't get shot this time?" Theodora asked innocently.

Chief White Crane laughed and said, "No, my child. Your crime doesn't warrant the death penalty." He paused and then continued, "But you would have to be chastised; the punishments we mete out fit the crime. Your privileges would probably be taken away for a month or two. You also would be given extra chores to do during that period of time."

Theodora returned to her lodge and Uncle Wilbur used this time to tell the girl about her ancestors.

"Your ancestors were slaves," he began. "They were beaten and whipped into submission just as you were. It was your iron will that kept you from betraying us to the enemy."

"Why do people have to be so cruel?" Theodora asked, disdain in her voice.

"It is the nature of man. Unless a person repents and turns his life over to Christ he is capable of such cruelty," Wilbur explained. "Even after turning to Christ it is impossible to live a perfect life because of our sin natures. God knew this so He made a way for us to become perfect in His eyes. He sent a substitute, His Son Jesus, to take the death penalty for us. Jesus did that when He took our sins on the cross. When someone believes and receives the Savior, Jesus' sinless nature is applied to his life. Those of us who are believers are sealed until we get to Heaven. This is when we will attain true perfection. Right now God sees us as perfect even though we are not because He looks at us through the blood of Jesus."

This was a lot for a fourteen-year-old to take in but Theodora understood in part. Right now she would share her frightening adventure with others in the village, not in order to entertain them but as a warning never to disobey the laws of the tribal leaders.

Chapter Eighteen

Training

Theodora and her Uncle Wilbur were called into a meeting at the tribal council a few weeks later. The girl wondered what she had done wrong now. Citizens of the village weren't usually called before the council unless they were about to be disciplined over some infraction.

The chief was smiling, however, when they stood before him. "I have called you here because we have made a decision concerning Theodora."

"What is it?" Theodora was all ears now. Could this have something to do with her future? She was about to hear the answer to her question.

"After much deliberation and prayer the counsel and I have sensed the Lord has some plan for Theodora," Chief White Crane continued.

"Can you tell us what it is?" Uncle Wilbur asked.

The chief cupped his hands and tapped his fingers together. Pausing briefly and with a pensive expression he continued. "We don't know what specific purpose God has in mind but it will be revealed at some time in the future. All He has told us for now is that she will need special training in order to be prepared for it."

"Special training? What kind of training?" Theodora had a very puzzled look on her face.

"You will see, Theodora. Tomorrow we shall begin." Chief White Crane looked first at Theodora and then Wilbur and smiled. "That is all for now. You may be excused."

After school the next day, Theodora met Joe White Feather outside the lodge on her way home. She and her friend, Nadine, had just finished straightening up the classroom.

"I am to be your instructor in the martial arts," Joe announced. He was a black belt karate champion, chosen by the council to begin Theodora's training. She was to be coached in both taekwondo and karate until she became proficient in both.

"I will teach you karate," Joe said. "That is a technique of self-defense which was developed by the Japanese. You will train for one hour every day. We will start now and afterward I will introduce you to Mike Standing Bull. He will instruct you in taekwondo which is a Korean form of this art."

Theodora worked hard with Joe for an hour as planned and then met her other trainer to begin her instruction in taekwondo. This was a routine that would continue every day except on Sundays.

"Why am I being taught these things?" Theodora asked Johnny one day when he had finished enjoying the evening meal with the White family.

"You are being prepared for the outside," Johnny replied.

Excitement welled up inside Theodora. "The outside!" she exclaimed. "Wow! You mean I will get to leave here sometime? I will be free to just come and go."

"When you are ready," Johnny responded.

"Oh I want to be ready. I can't wait to get out of here for a while and explore the world outside." Theodora was breathless with the prospects of all the adventure that waited for her just ahead.

"What will I be doing? Where will I be going?" Questions were shot like bullets at Johnny.

"Hold your horses," Johnny chided in a friendly manner. "I can tell you no more." Disappointment spread over Theodora's face.

"Don't look so downcast, girl. The time will be here before you know it, when you will be ready to leave here." With a smile, Johnny patted Theodora on the shoulder and then turned to go home.

The training was rigorous and Theodora felt like giving up at times but her tenacity, coupled with the anticipation of what was to take place in the future, kept her going.

Along with the martial arts, Theodora was introduced to fire arms. She practiced shooting at a target every day. With all the extra activity, Theodora was still able to keep up with her studies. In fact she excelled at most everything she did and was able to graduate with honors. She was chosen valedictorian and had the honor of addressing her graduation class with a speech.

"We are so proud of you," Adeline told Theodora one day. She was busily kneading the dough with which she would shape into loaves of bread. The Cheyenne diet wasn't enough for the White family. They yearned for the cuisine they had been accustomed to when they lived in Topeka. Johnny enjoyed this food as well and wanted to learn how to prepare some of the tasty meals himself. Adeline gave him several recipes to try.

When the other natives found out Johnny was cooking white man's food they poked fun at him in a friendly way and called him "squaw man." Johnny knew they were kidding so he didn't mind. He just joked along with them.

On Theodora's eighteenth birthday, Adeline made a cake. Several of her friends as well as Johnny were invited to the party. Many of the natives who came never saw a cake like this before. It was the first time Adeline had baked one since coming to Chota. She had just begun preparing the foods the White family so enjoyed only a few months earlier. That was when she began a regular routine of baking loaves of luscious homemade bread. How Theodora loved the glorious smells of cooking and baking as she entered the lodge where she had lived for the past nine years! Now on this special day she deeply breathed in the wonderful fragrance and licked her lips in anticipation of the delectable feast that waited.

As time passed, the White family returned almost exclusively to the diet they had grown up with. The Cheyenne didn't mind though. They had grown to love the family and they respected their customs just as the Whites respected theirs.

Theodora enjoyed shooting with a bow and arrow as well as a rifle. She had learned so much about the Cheyenne ways over the years and she had grown to love them. With her inquisitive mind she was always ready to experiment with new things.

At the birthday party, Theodora allowed herself to be dressed like one of the Cheyenne women. She enjoyed pretending to be one of them. In return, Johnny donned his Western outfit complete with cowboy hat and boots. Everyone laughed in amusement. Theodora introduced her guests to some games she had grown up with. After that everybody went outside to play a few Cheyenne games.

A favorite Cherokee pastime was the netted hoop and pole game. A net made from buckskin lacing was stretched over a hoop which was made from a branch bent into a circle and tied together with rawhide. The hoop would be rolled along by one person while two others threw long darts at it. The one who managed to hit the hoop most squarely in the center scored a point. Theodora loved the game and she soon became quite adept at it.

There wasn't much time for games, however, as Theodora continued her rigid training for three more years. By the end of this time, she had earned a black belt in karate and was able to hold her own against all others who were skilled in the art. The years had flown by quickly and she was now prepared for the next step.

Chapter Nineteen

Introduction to the Underground

When she turned twenty one Theodora expected a big party but her life was just about to take a turn. Instead of a caravan of guests arriving at the house only Johnny showed up. This had been planned by Johnny and Wilbur a week before. It was to be a surprise.

"It's time," Johnny announced without coming inside. Wilbur exited the lodge bringing Theodora along with him.

"Where are we going?" she asked.

"You will see," Johnny smiled but he said no more. The three trekked through the village until they came to a path leading into the forest with a large sign that read, "No Entrance." Theodora knew what that meant. Everyone in the village knew. It was located on the opposite side of the community and neither Theodora nor anyone else dared go near it. A law had been passed many, many years ago, way before she and her family ever relocated in Chota. Theodora never knew the reason for this law and she was afraid to ask. It was forbidden for anyone to go beyond this sign. Anybody doing so would face grave punishment which in this case meant the firing squad.

Theodora almost choked with alarm and stopped dead in her tracks as they approached the dreaded sign. "Stop!" she yelled, shaking her head and shuddering.

"It's ok," Johnny smiled. "Don't worry! We have special clearance."

The girl hesitatingly and gingerly stepped forward. After Johnny tousled her hair and laughed, she smiled and boldly walked ahead with the men.

Through the forest they went and after about a mile they came to a clearing. Just ahead was a high hill, the front of it covered with moss and vines. Johnny walked up to it and pushed the vines away to one side. Theodora sucked in her breath when she saw a large titanium steel door. To the right of it was a panel with numbers on it. Johnny keyed in a code and the door slowly opened up on rollers.

When the three stepped inside, Wilbur's jaw dropped in amazement. Before him lay the most advanced electronic system he had ever seen. It was as though they had stepped into the 25th century. Theodora gasped as well, not believing what she saw.

"Wh..Wha...?" Wilbur exclaimed.

"Welcome to the Underground!" Johnny proclaimed.

"The Underground?" Wilbur repeated.

"Let me show you around and try to explain if I may," Johnny said. In their tour of the place they saw many men working at computers far more advanced than any Wilbur had ever seen. And he had seen many of them, having worked with them most of his life.

Wilbur and Theodora pointed to two humungous mechanisms on either side of the entrance to the cave. "Those are the generators," Johnny explained. "They are operated by solar batteries. They last for decades and hardly ever need to be replaced."

Johnny took them outside again and pointed towards the top of a high hill where eight powerful solar panels were situated out of sight and out of reach. "This is how the generators get their power, directly from the sun. It is all stored in the batteries so on days when the sun isn't shining the generators can still be powered," Johnny explained.

Wilbur was familiar with solar energy in the outside world but never anything like this.

Theodora and Wilbur learned that this wasn't the only underground site of this kind. There was one for each of the tribes which were scattered all over the nation. Each one was carefully protected and almost impossible for the enemy to find.

"This is pure genius," Wilbur remarked. "Who invented this?"

"Let me introduce you to him," Johnny answered. "We are fortunate to have the man with us. This site is the oldest one and it was here when all of it began."

Johnny led Wilbur and Theodora over to an aged man with snow white hair. He sat in a cane chair and was bent over his work. "Meet Casper Warring Spirit," Johnny introduced. The old man looked up and smiled. "This man is 125 years old, the oldest man of all the tribes in America," Johnny continued. "And his mind is as sharp as ever. His IQ is 350 which far exceeds the highest one in recorded history."

"Quit bragging on me," Casper remarked with a sheepish smile. "I can do nothing apart from God. He is the One who gives me the ability to do what I do." He was always careful to give the Lord the credit for anything he did. His vast intelligence was matched by his humility.

"This is where we communicate with all the underground establishments," Johnny said. "We keep track of the NEWOPS and as much as possible the NWO as well."

"In order to retain our secrecy I developed a code that nobody has ever been able to break," Casper added.

"Soon you will learn this code and more," Johnny told Theodora.

"Why?" Theodora responded, wonder in her tone of voice.

"Because you are on the threshold of beginning to fulfill God's plan for this nation," Johnny said.

"What is it? Is this what I have been training for all these years?" Theodora inquired her eyes protruding with excitement.

"We are waiting for God's marching orders," Johnny answered. "He hasn't told us yet exactly what part you will be playing in all this."

Theodora was aware of the close walk with God that Johnny and the tribal leaders had but she was astonished at the way they could hear from Him in every detail. It was the kind of relationship Moses had with God when he talked to Him face to face. Theodora longed for a deeper relationship with the Lord that would enable her to hear from Him like that. She had been told that it took years of walking with Him to develop a keen spirit that would allow her to do that.

As they continued their tour of the establishment, Theodora learned that Johnny held a very high position in the Underground. Each Underground site had its own leader and the heads of these would get together once a month over an advanced communication system. It was so tightly secured that it was nearly impossible for the most experienced hackers to break into. The genius of it was that if someone did manage to get into the system they would hear and see only a conglomeration of gibberish.

The Underground had a few hackers of their own and many of them managed to break into secure government systems. This kept them abreast of what the NWO was doing on the most part.

"What do you want me to do now?" Theodora asked.

"Now you just wait for further instructions," Johnny answered.

In the meantime Wilbur and Theodora were initiated into the Underground. Wilbur, with his experience in electronics, was assigned to help Casper Warring Spirit while Theodora waited to receive her assignment.

While the trio was still inside the cave, a familiar voice sounded over a screen. It was coming from a Navajo site. Wilbur and Theodora hurried over to the screen to see who it was. They were astonished to see it was Paul Betzler. He was in the Underground too and he worked in communications. Although he had run a gas station in years past, he had been a radioman in the Navy. He was very familiar with code and he knew that the Navajo language had been used as code during World War II because the Japanese were never able to break it. As a result, the Navajo tribal leaders were put in charge of communications.

"Does each tribe have their own particular job?" Theodora wondered.

"They do," Johnny answered. "Our network is like a well oiled machine. Everybody knows what the other is doing and we work in conjunction with one another."

Johnny scratched his head in thought and then continued, "I must warn you, however, that the divulgence of this place carries the death penalty. Neither you nor anyone else is exempt from it, not even me." A shocked expression crossed the girl's face as she realized Johnny meant what he said. She gulped as she pondered on the seriousness of it all.

"What is the Underground for?" Theodora continued after momentarily reflecting on Johnny's warning to them.

"We are the counterpart to the NWO," Johnny explained. "Long ago God began leading us in a path against that of the enemy. You see, the devil is devious but God is smarter yet. He thinks he can outsmart God but our Lord always stays one step ahead. After the revival among the Indian tribes, God began to speak to the chiefs. He showed them His plan little by little and as they obeyed He exposed more to them."

"They are like prophets then," Theodora surmised. "It is like the Indian tribes here are a counterpart to the Jews in the Old Testament. They are the chosen people of America." The girl's eyes lit up with this new hypothesis.

"You are correct," Johnny said. "There is an adage among the leaders of our peoples that Jesus visited them after He was resurrected. The gospel isn't new to us even though we drifted away from God and invented gods of our own. We have always been a very spiritual people and open to the gospel. We just got off on the wrong path until God brought us back a hundred years ago."

Theodora took in every word Johnny spoke and she buried these thoughts in her heart. As she waited for her marching orders over the days and nights ahead she would think on these things often.

Chapter Twenty

Paul Betzler

While Theodora was waiting for her orders to come, something sinister was about to happen in the hidden Navajo village not far from the town of Ruidoso, NM.

Paul Betzler was seated at his computer in the Underground Headquarters of the Navajo nation. He had been the head communications navigator for the past five years. Shortly after the White family had left Topeka, the NWO began confiscating small private businesses and Paul's was one of them. He decided the best thing to do after that was to pack up his family and head towards New Mexico where Johnny Fast Horse had made contact with a Navajo friend for him. Brian Sly Fox met Paul and his family when they arrived at a way station located in a secluded area of the forest. Snow covered peaks of the Sierra Blanca Mountains loomed in the distance. Brian showed them around and allowed them to get acclimated to their new surroundings. The four Betzler children were all excited about the adventure that lay ahead of them and they could hardly wait to find out how the Navajos lived.

After the usual two week orientation period, Brian took the Betzler family to Nizhoni, the Navajo village hidden deep within the Lincoln National Forest near Ruidoso. The name of the village meant "beautiful" in Navajo and it was tucked far away in the forest where it couldn't be easily located.

Just as the Cheyenne had done, these native people practiced the old ways of their culture. They lived in hogans, dome shaped houses with wooden frames and walls made with clay. Paul noted that all the houses faced the East. They were built this way so the natives could enjoy the sunrise in the morning.

The Betzlers had to get used to a diet of corn, beans, and squash that was grown on the farm land in back of the village. Several kinds of meat were also added to the menu. The Navajo raised sheep and goats, a major source of their meat which had been brought to them by the Spaniards in the 17th century. They also enjoyed venison and rabbit along with prairie dog.

The first day the Betzlers arrived at the village, they sat down to a meal of fried cornbread, beans, and mutton along with some grilled prairie dog. The family was happy with their meal that had been prepared by some of the women of the village until they came to the prairie dog. They thanked them for the meal while politely declining the prairie dog.

Years went by as the children learned the very difficult Navajo language as well as all the Navajo culture and history. Their parents found it too arduous to learn, however, so they remained with the English language. Fortunately, the Navajos were fluent in Navajo, English, and Spanish as their Cheyenne brothers were.

The children, being young, acclimated to their new surroundings quickly but Paul and Martha struggled with the new life and they yearned for the old one back in Topeka. They knew they could never return, however, so they made their best efforts to get used to this new way of life. It helped that the people were followers of Jesus just as they were and they attended the frequent prayer meetings and church services which were held in a large log building. There was another big building where school was held and a third one where the tribal council would meet.

The men wore their traditional dress of tunics with breech clothes tucked in at the waist which were held together by Concho belts. On their feet they wore high, boot like moccasins and on their heads leather caps. The women wore skirts and blouses and their long hair was worn in a knot that was wrapped in white yarn. Yucca fiber and wool were used to make their clothing. During the winter the Navajo typically wore ponchos, cloaks and blankets. The women liked jewelry and most of their jewelry was made from silver and turquoise.

As the years passed, the leader of the village, Chief Iron Horse learned of Paul's talent and background in communication. Eventually the chief introduced Paul to the Underground which was located in a large cave outside the village. Further on was another large cave that would be used as a hideout in the event of an emergency.

After Paul had gained trust with the council elders, he was given a top security clearance and brought in as a member of the Underground.

Paul worked alongside his best friend, George Howling Wolf. They had been good friends for many years. George was an expert hacker who knew how to hack into government computers. Paul was the head communications man with a staff of twenty people under him. His job was to keep all the tribal leaders all over the country informed of any enemy movements that were taking place from day to day. George was a tremendous help to Paul because of his expertise in hacking.

This set up worked well and continued over the years. Then one day Paul's life fell to pieces. He was sound asleep in his hogan when two tribal militia men burst in without warning. They literally dragged Paul out of his bed. Martha woke with a start and cried out in a loud voice, "Paul, what is going on?" Before she knew it, Paul had been hauled out the door and into the tribal council building. There sat Chief Iron Horse along with the other tribal leaders.

Still half asleep, Paul spoke. "What's wrong? Why did you bring me here?"

"You are under arrest," the chief announced.

"But why?" Paul's face went pale and he began trembling all over. He looked around the room at the faces of each of the tribal men standing there.

"For treason," Chief Iron Horse answered grimly.

"That...That's impossible," Paul stammered.

"Take him away and lock him up," the chief ordered and two of the council members led Paul out. He was taken to a small cave with a barred door on the entrance to it. Inside was a cot and blanket along with a bucket for Paul to relieve himself in. On top of a small table was a basin with water along with a rag.

The next morning Paul was taken back inside the council building to stand trial. It turned out that he was accused of sending emails back and forth to the NEWOP headquarters that were located in Ruidoso. The evidence was damning as the emails revealed the fact that Paul had been collaborating with the enemy.

Brian Sly Fox was assigned to Paul to be his defense attorney. Paul felt more hopeful when he learned this because he considered Brian a good friend who would do everything he could to prove his innocence.

A jury had been selected and all that day they listened as the attorneys argued their cases before the judge. This went on for several days.

The night before the jury would announce their verdict in the case, Brian went to visit Paul in his cell.

"How do you feel it went today," Paul asked anxiously. "Does it look good?"

Brian shook his head. "No it doesn't, Paul. The prosecution has iron clad evidence against you. Is there anything at all you can think of that has happened over the last few weeks or months? If you can tell me anything that might help, I can make a final plea before the judge."

Paul shook his head glumly. "I have already told you all I know. If they find me guilty what will happen to me?"

Brian answered softly, "You will face a firing squad. I am sorry to have to tell you this; outside of a miracle I don't see any way out for you."

Brian paused and scratched his head in thought. Then he continued, "There is one more thing we could try, however."

"What is that?" Paul asked, hope rising in his voice.

"You could throw yourself at the mercy of the court," Brian suggested. "Maybe that way you could get a reduced sentence to life in prison."

That option didn't sound much better to Paul but it would at least give him more time to clear his name.

Morning came and a tribal policeman escorted Paul back to the council chambers where the final verdict would come down.

Brian stood before the judge and said, "I want to make a plea of mercy for my client."

Chief Iron Horse, the judge in this case, nodded his head affirmatively.

Brian proceeded in his plea, "Paul came to us several years ago from the outside world. He had to learn the ways of our people and become familiar with our laws. Because he is an outsider and new to our ways I am pleading for clemency so that his sentence, if found guilty, could be reduced to life imprisonment."

The chief answered gravely, "The law is clear. Treason is punishable by death. We can't make any exceptions. The lives of our people are at stake. We can't tolerate such a serious breaking of the law." He pounded a piece of wood which served as a gavel on the bench he sat at.

Paul lost all hope as he watched the jury walk back in. He knew in his heart that the verdict wouldn't be good. When the judge asked for it, each member of the jury stood up and one after another spoke the word "Guilty."

Paul cried out in anguish, "I'm innocent...innocent."

Chief Iron Horse gave Paul a chance to regain his composure. Then he stood and asked Paul to approach the bench. Paul stood sadly looking at the judge as he listened to the fatal words. "You have been found guilty by your peers. Therefore in one week from today you will be taken out to the firing range where you will be shot to death by a firing squad." Martha, who was in the room to hear the sentence, began wailing loudly. Brian gently escorted her out and everyone else was dismissed.

During the final days before Paul's execution, many tears were shed as he embraced and kissed his wife. They couldn't believe this had happened to them. It was like a nightmare from which they couldn't awaken.

Paul wasn't afraid of dying. He knew that he would be with the Lord. It was the idea that his widowed wife would never know the truth. His children would live the rest of their lives believing their father was a traitor. He bowed his head and prayed with bitter tears, "Oh God, I'm innocent. Why won't they believe me when I tell them I was framed?" Paul cried until there were no more tears left.

A key turned in the cell door and Paul looked up to see Brian entering.

"I'm so sorry that I couldn't do more for you, Paul," Brian said, placing a comforting hand on Paul's shoulder.

"I know you did all you could and I want to thank you for that," Paul said, still wiping tears from his eyes.

"I just talked with the pastor and he will be along to see you soon," Brian promised.

"It's that time, isn't it?" Paul sniffled. "Tomorrow the week will be up and I will be facing the firing squad."

Shortly after Brian left, Pastor Lone Coyote arrived as promised. After spending some time in prayer, they celebrated the Last Supper for the final time.

"Thank you, Pastor," Paul sobbed with his arms around his comforter. "You don't know what that meant to me."

That night Paul slept peacefully for the first time since his arrest.

When morning came Martha came to see Paul for one last time. They only had an hour left before Paul would be taken out to the firing range. Martha tried to make her husband's last moments as pleasant as possible. She had brought him a special treat, one of his favorites – a blueberry muffin. Paul took it from her and thanked her. He didn't feel much like eating it but he did, out of respect for what she had done for him.

After Paul kissed her goodbye for the last time, he looked squarely at his wife and said, "Please believe me when I say I am innocent."

Martha nodded her head and affirmed, "I do believe you, Paul. I know that in my heart." With a tear beginning to slide down her cheek, she turned and left, never looking back.

At 8:00 AM, two tribal policemen came and took Paul out to a forest clearing away from the village. This was a firing range which was also used as the place of execution. Here Paul was taken to a pole where he was tied securely with his hands bound behind his back. Paul looked around to see five expressionless militia men standing at attention, each with a rifle in his hand.

Years ago tribal leaders decided that the firing squad was the quickest and most merciful form of execution. Five of the best marksmen would be chosen for this unpleasant job. This was in order to avoid missing the mark, causing the condemned person to suffer needlessly.

The peace that Paul felt the night before disappeared as reality came crashing down around him once more. Fear gripped him as he looked at his executioners and he began pleading with God.

"Oh, dear God," Paul prayed as fresh tears began falling. "Isn't there something You can do to rescue me? Please, merciful God, please!"

As Paul continued to pray silently he felt a blindfold being placed over his eyes. With dread, Paul listened for the final orders of the tribal member. "READY!" came the command.

Paul's thoughts turned to his sweet wife, Martha, soon to be left a widow, devastated and heart-broken. He so wanted to hold her in his arms one last time. His only comfort right now was that he would see her again in Heaven some day along with his children.

"AIM!" Paul's heart skipped a beat as he heard the rifle bolts being pulled back. He squeezed his eyes tightly shut underneath his blindfold which was now soaked with his tears and sweat. Frantically he twisted his hands back and forth in their leather bindings in a last ditch effort to free himself, even though he knew it was useless.

Time seemed to stand still for Paul as he braced himself, waiting for the final command that would send the deadly missile through his chest right into his heart.

"FIRE!" came the command.

Just as the men were beginning to press the triggers of their rifles, Paul heard someone running towards them with a shout. "Halt! Don't shoot!" The men lowered their guns and looked towards the voice. It was Brian Sly Fox with a notice in his hand from the chief. The squadron leader took the message and read it.

"Release this man," he ordered. Immediately they untied Paul and removed his blindfold.

"Follow me," Brian directed and Paul shakily walked after him back to the village.

Still shaking from his frightening ordeal, he followed Brian and the others back to the Council Building. Chief Iron Horse sat there on his buffalo rug smoking a pipe. When he saw Paul he smiled broadly. "We caught the real criminal," he announced. "I want to apologize to you with all my heart. We nearly executed an innocent man."

Half crying with relief and gratitude, Paul smiled weakly and responded, "I know you meant well. You felt obligated to follow the law. I don't hold any of it against you. I am just happy to still be alive. Most of all I am glad that I don't have to worry that my children will be left believing their father was a traitor."

Paul caught his breath and after a brief pause he continued, "Who is the guilty one and how did you discover it?"

"This one was caught hacking into one of the other men's computers at the Underground," the chief replied. George Howling Wolf was brought in by two of the militia men. "He has confessed to everything."

"Not you, George! It can't be," Paul gasped. "Why? I thought you were my very best friend."

"I was always jealous of you and when you got promoted ahead of me I was very angry at you. I just wanted to get even is all. At the time I didn't think they would kill you." George choked up with tears. "I'm sorry. Please forgive me!"

Paul felt compassion towards George even though he had every right to be very angry with him. He had nearly cost him his life and ruined the lives of his family as well. But the love of Christ filled his entire being and it flowed out towards George.

When George was sentenced to death, Paul pleaded with the council to lighten his sentence. But the law was the law and it couldn't be changed. This was the tribal way. Paul went home to his wife who shed tears of joy at his release.

Paul found out how George had hacked into his and other people's computers. With his extraordinary abilities he figured out how to steal passwords on the most secure machines and then break into them using other people's names. This was how George was able to frame Paul. Paul's name had been fraudulently placed on the emails that had been sent to the NEWOPS. The council members were flabbergasted at how this could possibly be done. So they immediately contacted Casper Warring Spirit in Chota to inform him of the security problem and that he needed to develop a more secure system.

Paul went through the next few days feeling a mixture of joy and grief. He would carry in his heart the sorrow over the death of his friend for months. He hoped that George made himself right with God before going to his death before the firing squad. There was no way to really know. He could only hope that someday he would meet George in Heaven.

Chapter Twenty-one

Marching Orders

During the long wait for her unknown assignment, Theodora spent many hours in the cave of the archives. She had come upon an ancient history book with the title "History of the United States." With a ravenous hunger to learn the truth about the country, she devoured it and then read it over and over again. Each time she examined the text something new would stand out to her. Why hadn't anyone ever told her about this? Perhaps they didn't know. There were no volumes around except for here in this cave and perhaps a few other ones like this. Except for those that had been hidden away there were none to be found anywhere since the great book burning scores of years ago.

Theodora was amazed to learn that people actually elected their leaders and that there was a Senate and House of Representatives. The people were free and there was a U.S. Constitution that protected their freedom. There was freedom of speech, freedom of the press and freedom of religion under the First Amendment. In the back of the history book was a copy of the Constitution. Theodora studied each one of the Amendments carefully.

"What happened to our country?" she asked Adeline one day.

Adeline motioned for the girl to sit down with her. "Have some coffee, child, and I will tell you all I know."

Adeline proceeded to tell Theodora all she had been told from her grandmother who in turn learned from her grandmother the great truths about America in the days when the nation was still free. One of the biggest problems she was told was that Christians failed to get involved and to vote when elections rolled

113

around. The church separated themselves from the government which allowed secularism to take over. It was never meant for this to happen.

The Constitution was set up for the church to be protected from government intrusion. When people began to believe the lie about "separation of church and state" this began the ride down the slippery slope which led to the condition people were facing now. Before Christians knew what was happening, prayer and the Bible were removed from the schools. They began losing their freedoms one by one until things got so bad they were forced to do things against their consciences lest they be fined or imprisoned. Soon after that, churches, Christian schools and colleges were shut down. Even home schooling was outlawed.

"Now we aren't even allowed to hold prayer meetings in our homes," Adeline sighed. "All these things have occurred since the United States gave up its sovereignty to the UN. Eventually the UN morphed into what is now the New World Order Government or the NWO. The only people who are free now are those who bow to the rules and regulations of the new government. Of course we as Christians can't do that. Doing so would be breaking God's laws."

"You see," Adeline continued, "most of the fault of the nation's decline lies at the doorstep of the church. Now it's too late to do anything about it?"

Or was it? God was now ready to introduce Theodora to His latest plan.

Johnny Fast Horse knocked on the door just as Adeline had finished her last sip of coffee with Theodora. Wilbur stepped out of another room to answer it.

"Have I got news!" Johnny began.

"What is it?" Wilbur asked, motioning Johnny to sit down. Adeline brought him a cup of steaming coffee from the kitchen along with some fresh cookies she had just finished baking. Johnny had developed quite an appetite for her sweet morsels.

"We found out the President's press secretary was fired. Now he is looking for another one," Johnny informed. With that both he and Wilbur looked over at Theodora.

"You have had a lot of training and a great aptitude in correspondence," Uncle Wilbur mentioned, making a gesture towards the girl.

"Oh no," Theodora said shaking her head. "I know what you are thinking and the answer is 'No'."

"Just hear me out," Johnny said. He paused and then continued, "This will be your 'In' with the Underground in Washington DC. We took you into it because we knew you had all the makings of a good undercover agent. This would be a perfect place for a 'Plant' and there would be no one better than you to fill that job."

"It's too dangerous," Theodora protested. "Besides they would find out who I was immediately. I would be executed."

"But what if this is God's open door, the very assignment He has prepared you for?" Johnny argued.

"And what if it isn't?" Theodora countered.

"Ok! Let's put it to a test," Johnny suggested. "If after sending in your resume you don't get the job, we will know it isn't God's plan for you then. If you do get a positive response from the White House, then we can be pretty sure it is God's will for you to go."

Theodora nodded her head weakly and relented, "I suppose I can't argue with that one. After all I have been told all my life that God has a special plan for me. Besides the chances of my getting the job is one in a hundred million. I feel pretty safe." The girl smiled as she thought she had wiggled out of that one. But in obedience to her elders, she typed up a resume on her computer and emailed it to the proper recipients in Washington DC.

A security system had been built into the computer so any correspondence going out from it would show another location. Nobody would be able to find out that it had come from Chota or any other place close to it. Theodora was thankful for Casper Warring Spirit. In fact she planned to go over there with a plate of cookies when she had finished and thank him in person.

After Theodora had clicked the "Send" button on her computer, she gathered up a dozen still warm cookies from the kitchen and wrapped them up in a soft deerskin to take over to Casper's lodge. It was evening now so he would be at home.

Casper was always delighted to see Theodora. "You keep yourself too scarce," the old man said as he bit into one of the cookies.

"I've been busy," the girl remarked. "If it is in God's plan, I could be leaving here soon."

"Why, child, where are you going?" Casper asked.

"This is top secret but I know you have clearance so I can tell you," Theodora said. She knew that everyone else was way out of ear shot so she proceeded to tell him about the plan. "I just hope that I don't hear anything from Washington," the girl admitted.

"If this is God's will for you, my child, nothing can stop it so you must be prepared for whatever happens." Casper wiped the last bit of cookie crumbs from his mouth with his handkerchief and swallowed.

Theodora nodded in agreement and then after their chat, she rose to leave.

Two weeks passed and Theodora hadn't heard anything and as each day went by she felt more and more relieved. "God wouldn't send me into a lion's den," she thought to herself. "He has a much better plan than that, one that will keep me perfectly safe." Just as that last thought had gone through her head, she heard a knock at the door. It was Johnny and he motioned for her and Wilbur to go with him. When they neared the Underground cave, Theodora's heart began beating rapidly. She didn't have a good feeling about this at all.

Inside the cave, Johnny told them that they had received a message from Washington over the main computer. Because of the high security any emails coming into the Underground went to a false email address. From there, they were fed into a secure system and sent on to the people to whom they were addressed. This email had already been spit out to Theodora's computer which was sitting on her desk. As she read it, her countenance fell. The message was ordering her to come to Washington for an interview with the President. She had to concede that this was God's will for her. She had agreed to it when it was put to the test. Now she had no choice but to obey.

Johnny took Theodora into another room of the cave where she saw several flesh colored belts. They came in a wide variety of shades. Johnny held one belt after another next to Theodora's skin until he found a perfect match. The girl was amazed that the bands were so incredibly thin. They were no thicker than a napkin. "This is so it can be worn under your clothing without being detected by a scanner or frisking," Johnny explained.

"Here," Johnny continued. "Take this. You must keep this with you at all times. It is to be hidden inside the belt." He handed her a small iPhone that was as thin as tissue paper but was as firm and strong as a piece of titanium steel. It would fit perfectly inside the specially made belt. At the bottom of the iPhone was a button. When it was pushed the compact iPhone expanded into an eight by twelve inch piece of equipment.

Theodora's mind wasn't able to grasp such wonder. "Did Casper invent this too?" she asked. Johnny nodded. Theodora examined the iPhone closely and noticed another button that turned it on and off.

"It can do many things," Johnny said. "You can do everything ordinary iPhones can do and much more. The battery in it doesn't need to be recharged for ten years. And it is totally secure. Nobody will be able to break into any messages you send either orally or through the email."

"I don't understand how that can be done," Theodora said, scratching her head.

"Casper invented something else too. He managed to develop an internet of our own which is hidden within the main grid," Johnny declared. "And nobody will be able to detect it. It's a work of genius." This information almost blew Theodora's mind away. She felt like she had just stepped into another universe, a world of science fiction.

"Now go home and get a good night's sleep. A big day waits ahead of you," Johnny concluded.

Chapter Twenty-two

Stepping Into the New World

"You never told me how they won't be able to find out who I really am," Theodora mentioned to Johnny as he drove her to a secluded place where a private jet was waiting.

"We have been working with an underground agent who is located at a secret base near Washington," Johnny replied. "He is an expert hacker and has erased all information about you and your family from all the computers. Your name is now Theodora Blackwell. Remember that."

Johnny took his handkerchief and wiped his forehead, then continued, "From now on every document, every letter, every piece of literature must be signed using that last name. Do you understand?" Theodora nodded.

"Even when you contact us here back home, don't forget to use that. Your uncle has been placed on the most wanted list at the NWO. In order to safeguard you, we don't want anything that could possibly connect you to him. This means you can't ever contact him directly. You must always go through us and we will give you his false identity to use. You must refer to him as Wilbur Cleveland. Keep all I tell you in your head. Don't write any of this down. The less you write about any of this, the less likely you will be discovered for who you really are."

"I understand, Johnny," Theodora affirmed. "Thank you for all you have done for me and my family. I will never forget that."

"We will keep you in our daily prayers always," Johnny promised as the jeep came to a stop at a forest location 50 miles away from Chota. There was a small hidden airport here with a plane all equipped and ready to take off. Theodora boarded the small aircraft and was soon on her way.

The plane landed on the running strip of a small airport located 40 miles from Spruce Nob, WV. It was buried deep within the forest of the Alleghenies. As Theodora stepped off the small jet, she was greeted by a man who was dressed casually in a pair of jeans and flannel shirt. He wore a baseball cap on top of his partially balding head and looked to be in his mid-forties. "I'm Clifford Baldwin," he introduced. "I take it you are Theodora." Theodora nodded. She was dressed in a plain skirt and blouse with a blue scarf tied around her neck. On her feet was a pair of ordinary walking shoes and blue stockings that reached to her knees. She had left all her Cherokee wardrobe back in Chota. Now she would blend in nicely with the Washington citizens.

"I will show you where you will be living," Clifford said. Theodora entered a grey-colored jeep to begin the four hour ride to her apartment. Clifford told her the vehicle had been specially made so it wouldn't stand out too much. Theodora noticed the NWO license plates on the jeep and learned that they had been forged.

"You guys think of everything, don't you," Theodora remarked.

"We have to," Clifford stated, "in order to ensure our people's safety." As the jeep traversed its way down the windy roads to the main highway, Clifford began to fill Theodora in about her new assignment.

"Our agency is called Operation Dove," Clifford began. "We have 100 of our undercover agents working in and around Washington. I have been assigned to you and will be working closely with you during the time you are here. Our headquarters is stationed 35 miles outside Washington in a secret underground location. From there we will be working with you and protecting you as best we can. Our scanners will be on you at all times so you can feel secure with the knowledge you will never be left alone in the lion's den."

Clifford paused for a few moments and then laughed, "Don't look so serious. We typically call Washington the lion's den around Headquarters. That's our little inside joke."

"Oh!" Theodora exclaimed but didn't think that little joke was particularly funny. She would soon feel like she had been placed in with a bunch of hungry lions.

Clifford and Theodora walked through the door of her apartment. There were cameras and scanners placed in all corners of the room. All the walls were painted with an ivory color. On them were pictures of scenery and flowers, purposely placed there in order to make Theodora feel more at home. A pleasant scent of lilac wafted through the air. The peaceful atmosphere put Theodora more at rest.

As Clifford and Theodora sat on chairs next to the kitchen table, Clifford continued with the orientation. "These cameras make your apartment appear empty even when you are here. Nobody except us can ever see or hear what you say or do in here. The scanners allow us to see you and we have bodyguards ready to come to your rescue in the event of trouble." Theodora breathed comfortably knowing she would be as safe as possible.

"Now let me take you for some lunch," Clifford offered. "I know a good Chinese Restaurant you will enjoy." Theodora's mouth watered. She hadn't eaten Chinese food since leaving Topeka but she remembered how delicious it was.

As the pair sat enjoying a scrumptious lunch, Clifford continued his briefing. In the morning he would drive her to her first interview with the President. A lavender dress all pressed and ready was waiting back at the apartment along with a pair of spike heels and hose. Everything she needed was available. She had been instructed not to pack anything for the trip so the only clothes she brought was what she was wearing.

An assortment of dresses, skirts and blouses of varying colors and lengths hung in the closet. There were also some comfortable casual clothes consisting of blue jeans, slacks, blouses and sweaters. The dresser in the room contained lingerie and on top was a jewelry box filled with an assortment of jewelry – earrings, necklaces, and bracelets along with a couple of rings.

One of the rings had a transmitter in it so Theodora could contact Clifford at any time she needed him. There were two buttons on the ring she could push to engage the transmitter. One would reach Clifford and the other one a couple of body guards who were assigned to her in the event of an emergency. There was also a bottle of her favorite perfume sitting alongside the box.

"Johnny must have told Clifford about this," Theodora thought to herself. "How else would he have known what I wanted or needed?"

That night, Theodora had a difficult time falling asleep. She was anxious about the interview. Her mind was filled with visions of what the President might look like. Was he handsome? Was he tall? Theodora smiled sheepishly to herself. "I mustn't think such thoughts," she scolded herself.

Chapter Twenty-three

President Matthew Warner

It was the middle of the night and Theodora finally drifted off to sleep when she heard a commotion just outside her door. She reached for her lamp and snapped the light on just in time to see three NEWOPS burst into the room. She stood up to face them. As they tried to grab for her, she dodged this way and that striking with her feet and jabbing with her hands in karate chops, knocking one of them to the ground.

After about five minutes of running around and fighting with the NEWOPS, one of them managed to get behind her and grab her arms. Before Theodora knew it her hands were secured behind her in handcuffs.

"You are coming with us," one of the NEWOPS declared.

"Why? What am I being arrested for?" Theodora demanded.

"You should know...for being a spy," growled the NEWOP. Theodora was dragged roughly away, shoved into a police car, and whisked away. The vehicle stopped in front of a brick building a couple of miles away. Again the girl was manhandled as she was jerked out of the car and hauled inside the detention center.

Theodora soon found herself in a room with a bright light. The walls were stark white and the only furnishings in it were a table with straps on it and a chair. She looked in horror at it as she recognized it for what it was. She had been brought here to be executed.

Theodora struggled for her very life as she was ruthlessly dragged over to the table. The men were strong and every attempt to escape was futile. One of them strapped her down on the table while another picked up a syringe that had been filled with a lethal liquid. As the man approached the girl she saw pure evil in his eyes. Theodora struggled violently against the restraints.

"That won't do you no good so you might as well lie still," the man said, his lips curled in a jeer. He began toying with her as a cat with a mouse, waving the deadly syringe back and forth above her face, laughing sadistically all the while.

After a few minutes of cruel torment, the big NEWOP finally jabbed the needle into Theodora's arm. She screamed loudly over and over as she felt the deadly fluid flow through her veins. At last she quit struggling as her life began ebbing away.

With a gasp, Theodora jerked herself to an upright position. "Where am I?" she wondered. There was a soft glow in the room. "I must be in Heaven." Then she realized it was the nightlight and she was sitting up in her own bed.

She wasn't dead. In fact she was very much alive. Her nightmare had been so real. Was God trying to tell her something through that dream? What could it mean? Was He showing her how she would die? She shook her head then. God wouldn't be that cruel. He must have had a loving purpose in sending her that dream.

As she was wondering over the dream, she heard a knock on her door and her blood ran cold. "They've caught me! Perhaps my nightmare is about to become reality," she thought.

"It's me, Clifford," the voice said. Theodora breathed a deep sigh of relief and looked at her clock. It was 6:00 AM. "Oh no!" she exclaimed. "I must have overslept. In the excitement of meeting the President today I forgot to set my clock. I will be out in a jiffy."

Theodora tore around the room brushing her hair, applying make-up and shoving on her dress, shoes, a pair of earrings and a bracelet. She sprayed on some perfume and was out the door in a flash to greet a waiting Clifford. "I'm so sorry," she apologized.

The door led to a passageway which led to another door a block away. This one opened up to a subway system. From here they walked about another block to a set of stairs that led outside towards Clifford's jeep.

As part of her security, this method of entering and exiting Theodora's apartment was used. That way nobody would be able to see her directly coming to or leaving her residence.

"Your apology accepted," Clifford said, "but we have no time to waste. It is a 40 minute drive to the White House from here."

When they arrived, Clifford parked the jeep in a lot reserved only for official government employees. Besides being a secret agent, Clifford worked as a security guard inside the White House. "Some genius must have thought all this up so the undercover agents were able to work under the noses of the NEWOPS without being detected," Theodora surmised to herself. She thought about Casper Warring Spirit. Maybe he was the one who thought up all these clever ideas.

Soon Theodora found herself standing in the Oval Office before a man sitting at a large desk. He was poring over some papers which were stacked in front of him. Everything looked just as they had appeared in the pictures Theodora had seen in an old history book except for a couple of things.

The President's seal had been changed from the traditional one which featured an eagle with a branch in one talon and arrows in the other. Now it was the seal of the NWO. Instead of the American flag there was a red flag with a white circle in the center and inside it were three black sixes. It looked very similar to the Nazi flag of many years ago. The only difference was that flag contained a swastika instead of the sixes.

The flag of the NWO symbolized man at the center of all things, usurping God's throne. This was what the NWO stood for. Looking at this flag and seal made Theodora shudder.

The man at the desk finally looked up at Theodora. He smiled and stood up to introduce himself. "I'm President Matthew Warner." She was intrigued by how handsome he was, even more that she had imagined. She was also surprised at his race. He was the second black man to hold the office of the presidency in U.S. history. She reached out her hand to meet the President's and he shook it firmly. "Please sit down," he offered and Theodora sank down into one of the luxurious stuffed chairs which was situated near the desk.

"Where are you from, Theodora?" President Warner asked.

"I'm from Coldwater, OH," she replied. She had been instructed by the Underground to say that, when asked, in order to mask her true identity.

"Tell me about your family," the President continued.

"I have none. I was orphaned as an infant," Theodora answered. She had partially told the truth because her birth parents had been killed. She just left out the part about her being adopted by Pastor William White and fortunately she wasn't asked about that.

Everything that had been connected to Theodora, her adoptive family and her background had been erased from all the government computers and replaced with false information by Johnny's hacker friend in Washington. What had been added to the computers was false information which depicted her as a university graduate who had studied to be a correspondent.

Theodora was very careful to answer the President's questions in a way so as not to give away her secrets.

Satisfied with her answers, the President stood once again. "I will be in contact with you again," he said smiling.

"Do I get the job then?" Theodora asked, her face brightening.

"I will let you know. I have some more interviews to do," the President answered. Theodora left to return to Clifford's jeep and back to her apartment with mixed feelings. Part of her wanted the job and the other part was afraid of it.

"I don't understand the way this government is set up," Theodora wondered as they drove back.

"The world has been divided into ten regions now," Clifford explained. "This had been planned a long time ago, way before either of us was born, by a group called the Club of Rome. We once had a United Nations but when that failed to bring permanent peace to the world, it was eventually dismantled and replaced by the NWO. The world had been in turmoil with civil wars and terrorist attacks everywhere. When a limited nuclear war broke out in the Middle East it was decided a central system of government was necessary in order to quash the unrest in the world."

Clifford cleared his throat and then continued, "The NWO was put in place and a President was selected by the previous UN leaders. He has authority over all the Presidents, Prime Ministers and Kings who are in command over the ten regions. Actually they are mere puppets because it is the World Leader who pulls all the strings. However the regional leaders have been given quite a bit of authority over their own citizens. President Warner has command over all of North America which includes Canada, the United States, and Mexico. Each region has its own dictator so to speak and each one flies the NWO flag."

127

"Is there any way this will ever change?" Theodora asked.

"This is why we are here — to keep one step ahead of what the NWO is doing. Through much prayer and guidance along with any knowledge we can gain, we believe that eventually this evil system will be brought down," Clifford continued. "Three of the regions have weak leaders. President Warner is one of them. This is why you have been placed here in the White House. Your job is to try and win the President over to our side."

"I don't know if I can do that? I'm afraid," Theodora admitted.

"As a security guard I will be able to keep you protected. I will always be close by so I can continually keep a close watch on you," Clifford assured. He patted Theodora's hand comfortingly and she remained quiet for the rest of the drive back.

"I know this job won't be easy but you wouldn't be here if I didn't think you were up to it," Clifford continued. "God is on your side and I believe you are here for such a time as this." These words were familiar to Theodora. It reminded her of a Bible story her grandmother once told her, a story about another girl who had been chosen for a special purpose.

"Could this be why I am here?" Theodora wondered to herself. The mystery was beginning to unravel in her mind.

Chapter Twenty-four

Close Call

Theodora grew restless while she was waiting for word from the President so she decided to take a walk one evening. She knew better but her adventurous spirit caused her to throw caution to the wind. It had gotten her into serious trouble several years back but she didn't care. She was just plain bored. It would be fun to venture out and see a little bit of Washington DC without a body guard or Clifford tagging along.

Theodora dressed in a casual pair of blue jeans, a pink blouse and the same pair of walking shoes she had worn when she first arrived in the city. With a brush of her hair and a little application of lipstick, she was ready to go. She grabbed her jacket and purse and was soon out the door.

Theodora felt light and free as she walked through the passageway to the door that opened up to the metro. As she moseyed along, she thought she heard footsteps behind her. When she went faster, they kept right in step. When she slowed down, it was the same. Then she noticed no subways were running. It was 8:00 PM and there were no transits after 7:00 PM. Theodora had forgotten this. Panic began to rise up in her as she quickened her pace towards the steps leading out. Before she could reach them a pair of hands grabbed her pinning her arms behind her waist.

"I gotcha, gal, and you are going to give me what I want," a husky voice said.

Theodora screamed and managed to pull away after a solid kick to his groin, leaving the man doubled up in pain. She had remembered the tricks she had learned in her martial arts training.

Theodora started towards the stairs again but her attacker grabbed her again. This time she whirled around to face her adversary, her hands and feet in position for battle. Her enemy stood about 6' 2" tall and had a head of blond curly hair. He wore a worn overcoat and his face was covered with a scruffy beard and mustache.

Before Theodora could move, the man pulled a gun.

"You will come with me," the man growled. As he reached for her she kicked out at him again in an attempt to knock it out of his hand. The man anticipated her attack, however, and the gun went off. Theodora yelped in pain as a bullet passed through her abdomen out her left side. The man hesitated, leaving an opening for the girl to attack him again. Theodora became a flurry of hands and feet as she spun and kicked again and again. A well placed karate chop to the adversary's neck and another kick to his groin sent him reeling to the ground in agony. This time he didn't get up.

Grasping her wounded side, Theodora felt her blouse which was now drenched in blood; it soaked down into her jeans. As she staggered her way back through the tunnel she left a trail of blood. By the time she arrived back at her apartment, blood was pouring from her side. However she managed to make it to her bed before collapsing. Before losing conscienceless she was able to push both buttons on her ring. Soon two bodyguards rushed in with Clifford following close behind.

Clifford took one look at Theodora and then made a Code Blue call to the Operation Dove medical team. It wasn't five minutes when a doctor and nurse arrived.

The doctor gave Theodora a quick look-over and then commented sternly, "This girl is almost gone. We have to get some blood into her right away." He quickly took a blood test on the girl and everyone else in the room in order to find a match. It turned out that Clifford had the right blood type. The doctor took a rubber tube and needles which were attached at both ends and poked one into Clifford's arm. Then he took the other end and inserted it into the girl's arm. The life-saving blood began flowing from Clifford's body into Theodora's while the doctor made a call to the medical team at the Operation Dove Headquarters and ordered them to send four units of Type A blood ASAP. Soon a helicopter dropped off the hemoglobin.

Theodora woke up to tubes going in and out of her veins. They were connected to bags of life giving blood which hung above her bed. The first face she saw was that of Clifford. "You gave us quite a scare," he stated gravely. "We thought we were going to lose you for a while there."

"What happened?" Theodora asked. "I only had a flesh wound."

"That is true," the doctor said. "No vital organs were hit but the bullet nicked an artery on the way through your body. You must have done something to open up the artery because you were hemorrhaging badly," the doctor said. "I managed to get the bleeding stopped in time. Just lie still now. We had to give you five units of blood. You are all patched up now but you need rest. You won't be fit to move around for some time yet."

"Oh yeah," Theodora gasped. "It must have happened when I fought that guy." Her head was still feeling light from her loss of blood.

"Luckily the bullet went through your body at an angle. If it had gone straight through you wouldn't be here now," the nurse voiced.

Theodora began to feel strength coming back into her body and she drank some juice the nurse offered her.

"Just what were you thinking running out like that without even a body guard to protect you?" Clifford scolded. "You know better than that. You were lucky nothing worse happened to you. Did you know that two of our agents have been found out and executed by lethal injection just this month? There is no room for carelessness on this job."

"I'm sorry," Theodora said. "Believe me, it won't ever happen again." Theodora had learned a lesson she wouldn't soon forget. This incident coupled with her recent nightmare would serve as a reminder for a long time to come.

After apologizing profusely to the men, Theodora told them they were no longer needed and she would be fine. She remained in her bed, too weak for her nightly routine of showering or even brushing her teeth. It would have to wait until morning. Besides she didn't want to disturb the bandage that covered her wound.

She decided now would be a good time for her personal devotions; so she opened her compact iPhone to read a chapter from her E-Bible. This online Bible had been one Casper had prepared just for her. Actually it was just a makeover of a popular one which had been readily available over the internet until it was banned by the NWO. This Bible was safely hidden away on the secret internet within the main grid and it was beyond the reach of the enemy.

Theodora finished her devotions before settling down for the night. Her throbbing side would keep her awake for a while until the pain pill the nurse left for her took effect. When she finally drifted off into slumber she had pleasant dreams.

Chapter Twenty-five

Return to the White House

Two weeks passed and Theodora finally received word that the President wanted to see her. Now she was bustling about getting ready before Clifford arrived. She had just finished applying the last bit of makeup when the knock came.

A mixture of fear and excitement ran through Theodora on her way to the White House. After she arrived, she was met by a couple of security guards. Clifford was off duty this day so he wasn't able to join the entourage which accompanied her to the Oval Office. When Theodora appeared, the President was already waiting along with Vice-President Bora Findler. President Warner smiled at Theodora as she entered the room while Bora wore a dour expression, her hands defiantly planted on each hip.

"Sit down, Theodora," the President invited. Turning to his Vice-President he said, "You may leave, Bora." As Bora left the room, Theodora found a comfortable stuffed chair and sat down.

"Congratulations, young lady," President Warner announced. "You are my pick for press secretary."

Theodora was speechless.

"Well, what do you have to say to that?" the President smiled, picking up his pipe to have a smoke.

"I...I don't know what to say," Theodora stuttered. "I never expected to get picked for this job. All I can say is 'Thank you, Mr. President.'

"You can call me Matthew, Theodora. We are informal around here and, as my press secretary, you will be working very closely with me," Matthew informed. As they talked, the President filled Theodora in as to her duties. She would be responsible for collecting information about actions and events within the administration. She would conduct a daily press briefing to keep the media abreast of everything that was going on within the White House and the President's relationships and involvement with other governments around the world. Theodora would meet with the President each morning before setting out to the press conference.

Because of her position, Theodora was able to learn everything the NWO was doing. She cringed when she discovered how people were being treated. There were few people over 70 years of age who existed any more outside of the villages of refuge. No handicapped or unwanted children were around either. They had all been murdered by the NWO. Although the NEWOPS had eased up on raiding the house churches, Christians weren't allowed to say anything against the government. Those who dared do so were killed.

Theodora wondered about her loved ones back home. She hoped they were safe but she didn't dare try to find out lest they be discovered.

As she worked alongside the President she lost her fear of him. Bora, however, was another story.

Bora was a large woman, very husky, weighing around 225 pounds. She wore a beige skirt and jacket bearing the NWO insignia on the sleeve of the left arm. On her feet were plain black official looking shoes similar to those worn by soldiers during boot camp training. Around her neck she wore a black man's tie. This along with her short hair gave her a masculine appearance.

"I don't trust that girl," Bora complained to Matthew one morning after Theodora had gone to her press briefing.

"Why?" Matthew asked.

"You didn't choose her from one of the girls who have worked within the administration. Instead you go picking her

134

from the outside where she couldn't be properly vetted," Bora grumbled spitefully.

"Look, Bora," Matthew retorted. "Do you think I would have hired her if I hadn't thoroughly checked her out? Besides she attained her top secret security clearance, didn't she? What more do you want?"

"Alright, Matthew," Bora conceded. "But I still don't trust her. There is just something about her I don't like."

"Like what?" Matthew asked.

"She just seems too proper to me, too……" Bora's voice trailed off as she turned to leave the office.

"You are just too much," Matthew laughed as Bora opened the door to leave. Without responding to that last remark the Vice-President exited in a huff, shutting the door loudly behind her.

At the end of the day, Theodora returned to her apartment thoroughly exhausted. "Will it be like this every day?" she wondered. The information she was gathering concerning the NWO curdled her stomach. She didn't see how she could do the press briefings day after day without revealing the deep feelings of disgust and sorrow she carried inside.

She kicked off her spike heels and rubbed her feet. It felt so good to be rid of them for the evening. Then she undressed, hung her dress neatly in the closet, and put on something more comfortable before preparing her nightly meal. Wondering what to have, she explored her refrigerator and came across some chicken and asparagus. "That looks good," she thought to herself as she began frying the chicken in her electric fry pan. She began a pot of boiling water on the stove to put the asparagus in.

"I wonder what my grandmother is fixing right now," she thought to herself. She missed the meals and companionship of her family back home. As she thought about the many pleasant evenings with them she grew homesick. In her mind she could see Johnny seated at the supper table with them, enjoying the evening repast and sharing adventure stories from his childhood. "How I miss them all!" Theodora sighed as she thought about the simple, carefree small town environment in the village.

As the evening glow of the setting sun faded, Theodora got her iPhone out and sent an email to Johnny at the Underground Center near Chota. She told him about everything she was doing and how much she missed him and the family. She knew that he would relay the message to Adeline, Uncle Will and Aunt Edna. After pressing the "send" button, she turned on the TV screen and put a DVD into her player. She began watching a show from ages past, one which few people in this era had even heard of. It was "Leave It to Beaver." How she enjoyed these old humorous family programs! She grabbed some microwave popcorn she had just prepared and settled down to watch the relaxing program.

That night Theodora fell asleep to pleasant dreams once more.

Chapter Twenty-six

Interrogation

Several weeks had passed and Theodora went through her usual briefing with the President and then on to her meeting with the press. She wasn't aware of what was about to take place when she returned to the White House that evening.

It was around 4:00 PM and President Warner was out of the office. When Theodora arrived to share the day's events with him, Bora was waiting. She had a look of spite on her face which sent shivers down Theodora's back.

"Is anything the matter?" Theodora inquired.

"You come with me," Bora ordered, taking her roughly by the arm out the door, down the hall and to an elevator that led to the basement of the White House. They eventually arrived at a room with a couple of chairs and a table. Other than a picture of the NWO President and flag, the room was empty.

Bora sat at the table with Theodora seated opposite her.

"Just who are you?" Bora demanded.

"You know who I am," Theodora responded. "I'm Theodora Blackwell."

"Why don't I believe you?" Bora snarled. She rose and glared at the girl. Then she repeated the question.

Theodora was in tears and shaking. "I told you who I am. I have top secret security clearance. Isn't that proof enough for you that I am who I say I am?"

"You little twit," Bora shouted. "You better tell me the truth."

Theodora was thoroughly frightened. Why was this happening to her? Did Bora find out her true identity and the true reason she was here? She was trembling all over as Bora shouted question after question. There was nothing left for the girl to say so she remained silent.

Bora began slapping Theodora. The memory of her nightmare returned to her mind and she envisioned the three NEWOPS coming in to drag her off to be executed. She began sobbing as fear gripped her, tears sliding down her cheeks.

Suddenly the door opened and Theodora screamed in horror. To her relief it wasn't the three frightening men. It was President Warner.

"Bora, just what are you doing?" he demanded.

"Since you won't bother to find out who this girl is I am doing the job for you," Bora snapped. She held utter contempt for Theodora.

"Bora, we've been over this before. Now you let her go and get back to your office. Don't you ever bother this girl again, do you hear me?" Matthew threatened.

Obediently but begrudgingly, Bora let go of Theodora's arm. She turned to leave the room but not before shooting a scathing glance at the girl. After Bora was gone, Matthew placed a soothing hand on Theodora's shoulder and began speaking to her in a soft voice. "Are you alright, Theodora? Did she harm you in any way?"

Theodora shook her head. She had never seen him so angry. He always seemed so cowed by Bora before. In her bossy way, she would take over and demand her own way when it came to making decisions about how things were run around the White House.

Theodora looked up at Matthew now, admiration in her eyes. He was like a knight in shining armor, a hero who had just swept her off her feet. The fury in his eyes towards Bora was now replaced with a soft, gentle look as he spoke to Theodora. His personality was so different from Bora's. Bora was rough and uncouth, so difficult to be around. What made him so different from all the others around here? She couldn't recall a time when she felt threatened by him. Why was that?

From that day on, Theodora felt a fondness in her heart for the President. From the look in his eyes when he greeted her each morning, she felt that perhaps he was growing to feel the same about her.

As the days passed Theodora began to wonder if this was part of God's plan. After all, she had been sent to Washington by the Underground to be an influence on the President.

"No, this is impossible," Theodora disregarded that thought as she ended another day at her job. Now back in her apartment, she settled down to watch her favorite show "Leave it to Beaver."

Chapter Twenty-seven

The Operation Dove Headquarters

"The time has come for me to show you how we do things at Operation Dove," Clifford announced to Theodora one day.

It was Sunday and Clifford drove Theodora into a wooded area where he left his jeep hidden away from prying eyes. From there he took her to an underground tunnel where Theodora noticed several large tunnels with tubes running through them. Inside some of them were cars hooked together like a train. It was some futuristic kind of subway system of the sort Theodora had never seen before.

"What is this?" the girl asked in astonishment.

"This is our underground transportation system that leads to our headquarters," Clifford answered. With the push of a button he opened a door of the tube and invited Theodora to step into one of the cars within.

"Don't be afraid," Clifford assured, seeing Theodora's hesitation. He offered her his hand and gently helped her into the waiting car.

The car sped along in the vacuum tube at 200 miles an hour which took them to their destination within minutes.

"Our Sunday meeting begins in 30 minutes," Clifford told Theodora. "Before the service starts, we can have some coffee and donuts. I will introduce you to some of the brethren." Soon they entered a fellowship hall where they enjoyed some refreshments. After Theodora met Clifford's friends she was taken into a room that appeared to be a large sanctuary. It was equipped with the typical altar, pulpit, baptismal tank, and cross of the old churches Theodora had learned about. It even had a few stain-glassed windows with images of Christ and His Disciples.

Theodora was surprised to see a copy of the Bible sitting on top of the pulpit.

"Where did you get that?" Theodora asked Clifford.

"It is one of the few that had been hidden away by the Cheyenne Indian tribe many years ago," Clifford answered.

"I want you to meet our pastor," Clifford continued as he introduced Theodora to Pastor Luke Emerson. His countenance glowed with the beauty of Christ as he shook her hand. He reminded her of the father she had once known so many years ago.

After the church service, Clifford took Theodora to a dining area where everyone enjoyed a sumptuous meal. Theodora had many questions but Clifford told her to wait because he was about to show her the answers.

Clifford took Theodora to an enormous room in the headquarters where many computers were in operation. He introduced her to some of the operators who greeted her with a friendly smile and then continued with their work.

"This is just a skeleton crew today because it's Sunday. Ordinarily we don't work on Sunday but it is necessary to keep a small crew on because we have to stay in constant contact with all our affiliates located at all the refugee villages in the country," Clifford explained.

"Here at Operation Dove we feed information back and forth to all our Underground tribal subsidiaries," Clifford informed.

"Wow! This is huge," Theodora remarked.

"This way everyone keeps up to date on what is going on so nobody will be caught unaware of the goings-on of the NWO," Clifford smiled.

"I guess we can feel pretty safe then," Theodora said with assurance.

"Generally we can but there is always danger and we need to try to keep ahead of it at all times." Clifford drew out his handkerchief to wipe his nose. "As you already know two of our agents have recently been executed. Somehow the enemy manages to break through our security in some way. Most of the time, when an agent gets caught, it is due to carelessness on his part. He will either let something slip to someone he supposes is a friend or he will leave a piece of information lying around that draws suspicion. In this business you have to consider everyone your enemy, even me."

Theodora was surprised at these last words. If she couldn't trust Clifford, who could she trust? She remembered, then, what she had just read in her E-Bible the night before, how Judas, a trusted Disciple of Jesus, betrayed Him. She knew that her trust had to be in Christ alone.

"Are the Indian tribes in this country part of God's plan?" Theodora asked.

"I believe they very well could be," Clifford answered. "As God chose Israel to bring the good news to the world, why couldn't He have chosen the Indians to do the same thing here in these final days before our Lord's return? After all the Native Americans were the first to live here. America belonged to them before we came. Perhaps they truly are a counterpart to Israel."

"Maybe that is why the Holy Spirit was poured out on them first during the great revival of years ago," Theodora added.

"Yes and they remained committed to God even when everyone else fell back into the ways of the world," Clifford said. "This is why God can use the tribes today for His final plan."

"Yes, His plan," Theodora echoed. "And somehow God is fitting me into it. I still don't understand just how it is all going to work out though."

"You will when His perfect time is here. God has a way of revealing things to us just as we need them, just before they are to take place in His great scheme of things," Clifford smiled.

"So much to think and wonder about," Theodora remarked as Clifford led her back to the underground tunnel and into the car, waiting in the vacuum tube, to take them back to the jeep which would return them to Washington.

Chapter Twenty-eight

Death of a Saint

It was Friday evening and Clifford settled into his apartment after delivering Theodora back to hers. He had been on duty as security guard for the day and was happily looking forward to a weekend of leisure.

After eating the supper he fixed in his microwave, he settled down with his iPhone to send off a few messages to some of the key tribal leaders in the country.

Things had gotten heated up lately around the country as some people had banded together to revolt against the NWO. It wasn't Christians who were behind this but Clifford knew they would be the ones who would bear the blame. His spirit had grown increasingly uneasy and with this sense of foreboding he thought he had better warn the tribes to stay on high alert. There was just something in the air and he couldn't quite put his finger on what it was. Was the enemy about to attack in a new and furious way? Whatever it was, Clifford didn't feel good about it.

He went to bed and the feeling wouldn't leave him. He tossed and turned until about 2:00 in the morning when he heard something just outside his door. Without warning three NEWOPs burst into his room. They grabbed him and without letting him get dressed forced him out the door and into a waiting vehicle.

"What is this?" Clifford demanded.

"You think you spies can get away with it, don't you," one of the NEWOPS snarled.

Soon they arrived at a police station where Clifford, still in his pajamas, was hustled through a door. He was taken into a room painted grey from the floor to the ceiling. Not a stick of furniture was in the room except for a couple of chairs and a large light bulb hanging on a long cord down from the ceiling.

Clifford was pushed into one of the chairs and the interrogation began.

"Tell us where your headquarters are," one of the NEWOPS demanded, shining the bright light in Clifford's eyes. He was a hefty man, 6' 2" tall and weighed around 240 pounds. He was clean shaven except for a thick mustache. His bushy eyebrows that almost reached down to his eyes gave him a particularly villainous appearance. His features looked like that of a Swede with close set eyes and narrow nose in a broad face.

The other two NEWOPs weren't as large. One was around 6 feet tall, about 50 years of age and had a balding head. The other one was only 19 years old and was tall and lanky. The young one stood a way back from the other two.

Clifford remained silent under the questioning. Soon the big Swede began to hit him hard with his fists as he yelled over and over, "Tell me, spy! Tell me."

As the fists pummeled his face and chest for about five minutes, Clifford lost consciousness. He was awakened with a bucket of water splashing in his face.

"We will let you think about it for a while," the burly man said. Turning to the others he ordered them to take Clifford to his cell. He had suffered swollen, black eyes, a broken nose, some missing teeth and several fractured ribs.

Inside his cell, Clifford began praying, "Lord, help me to endure. Without You, I won't be able to keep from talking. Help me not to hate my captors." As he lay there, blood seeped from his mouth and nose and soaked into the tattered, thin prison blanket which was spread out on his cot. During the night the air grew cold in his unheated cell; Clifford grabbed the blanket from underneath him and clutched it around him in an effort to keep warm. His ribs ached and he occasionally coughed up blood from a punctured lung.

The ruthless beatings and torture continued for the next thirty-eight hours. During this time he was deprived of food, water and sleep. Clifford learned that the name of the Swede was Dutch Amundsen, the other one Thomas Rivers, and the youngest one Timothy Everest.

When Dutch saw that he wasn't going to be able to break Clifford, he growled at him, "There is only one thing left to do with you." Then he grabbed him by the arm and dragged him to another room. This room was stark white with only a table and one chair in it. The table contained several straps which were used to restrain the victims of the NEWOPs. As Clifford was being forced down onto the table, he began to speak through cracked and swollen lips. "You can destroy my body," he croaked, "but you can't touch my soul." Dutch glared at him in disdain.

As he was being strapped down, Clifford felt the presence of the Holy Spirit. His heart filled with Godly love and compassion toward his tormentors, he began to share the good news of the gospel with them. He told them how much God loved them and that He loved them so much He sent His only Son, Jesus Christ, to die in their place. If they would only turn to Him and receive Him into their hearts, He would forgive them and they would be able to spend eternity with Him. Clifford pled with them, telling them there was no hope outside of Jesus and if they didn't receive Him they would face an eternity in Hell.

Dutch mocked Clifford and Thomas smirked with unbelief because they were so entrenched in their false religion; their hearts were hardened against the truth. Timothy, however, stood silent and unnoticed in a corner of the room.

Dutch filled a syringe with a lethal fluid and then tied a band tightly aound Clifford's arm just above the elbow until a vein stood out. As the deadly chemical was being injected into his veins, Clifford cried out, "Father, forgive them for they know not what they do." Then he screamed in agony as the poison coursing through his body turned to fire.

Timothy watched as Clifford's body began to twitch in its final death throes. A tear leaked from the corner of one of the young NEWOP's eyes and silently rolled down his cheek. Because he was standing away from the other two, they never took note.

As Clifford closed his eyes in death, he opened them again to see a glorious figure dressed in a shining white robe. He immediately recognized Him as his Savior. While Clifford was gazing upon His beautiful face, Jesus stretched out His arms toward him and said, "Well done, thou good and faithful servant. Come and participate with Me in My joy."

It was now Monday morning back at Theodora's apartment and she was expecting Clifford to come knocking at the door any moment. She had just slipped on her heels, when the knock finally came. When she opened the door, she was surprised to see it wasn't Clifford. Instead it was another agent by the name of Ralph Winters.

"May I come in?" Ralph asked, his voice solemn.

"Sure, come on in," Theodora answered, concern in her voice. She sensed that the news she was about to receive wasn't good. It wasn't like Clifford to miss his appointment without first letting her know. Perhaps he was ill, she thought. She hoped that was all it was and he would soon be feeling better.

Ralph gently led Theodora to a table where they both sat down.

"I'm sorry I have to be the one to tell you this," Ralph began. Theodora knew right then that something horrible had happened to Clifford. "Clifford has been martyred. He was taken by the NEWOPS very late Friday night." After Ralph told her everything that had occurred, Theodora broke down in wracking sobs.

By this time five months had passed since she had begun her job at the White House. Theodora didn't feel up to going to work but she didn't know what excuse to hand the President. She decided it would be best just to tell him that she was ill and just let it go at that. When she finally told him via an email she received one back stating that he understood.

When Theodora was ready to return to work a couple of days later, she learned that Ralph had been assigned to take Clifford's place. He would be the one who would pick her up and take her home each day. Ralph was also a security guard at the White House.

Theodora didn't feel as secure any more since Clifford's untimely death. She kept wondering if she would be next. After all Clifford must have taken every precaution. What more could she do than he must have done? She would break down weeping each time she thought of Clifford. When she appeared at her press briefings it was all she could do to retain her composure.

At times she would begin to wonder if she had missed God's purpose by even being there. Then she remembered what Johnny Fast Horse and Clifford told her.

At night, Theodora thought about President Warner. Over the weeks and months she had developed tender feelings towards him. Perhaps there was another reason she had been placed there working alongside him.

Chapter Twenty-nine

Assassin

A month had passed and President Warner was in his office along with Vice-President Findler. The President was puffing on his pipe as he and the Vice-President were going over some business. Two security guards entered, dragging another man with them.

"What is this?" the President demanded. "Why are you bursting in here like this?"

"This man was conspiring to assassinate you, Sir," one of the guards said.

"Oh!" President Warner expressed shock. "Where did you find him?"

"He was caught sneaking around on the White House grounds. When we searched him we discovered he didn't have a pass to show he had the proper clearance to be there," the guard answered. "After about an hour of interrogation he confessed to a plot to assassinate you, Mr. President. Here is the gun we confiscated from him." President Warner took the gun, looked at it and then set it down on his desk.

"Lock him up," Bora piped up. "I will tend to him myself later. You can be sure he will be executed but first I want to talk to him. I need to find out how he got here and why the security was so poor that he was able to get this far."

The President, visibly shaken, took his seat at his desk. "Yes, Bora, how did security get so poor? Aren't you the one who is in charge of it?" He looked up at her, anger in his face.

"I...I don't know," Bora answered. "Something somehow slipped through my fingers. After all, sir, I can't be everywhere at all times. These things happen."

"Well you had better tighten things up around here, Bora. This better never happen again or I will have your head." It wasn't like Matthew to stand up to Bora like this. Before Theodora had come to work for him, he never had the backbone to do this. It was like their roles were reversed in the past. Somehow Theodora's presence gave him a boldness he had never had before. Had she done something to his heart as well?

Bora left the room and President Warner paced back and forth as he was drawn deeply in thought. "What is it about Theodora?" he asked himself. "She is so different from everyone else around here. She is kind and gentle. She is also beautiful, the most beautiful woman I have ever seen. When she enters the room, my heart skips a beat. She absolutely makes my day. I would never want to see anything bad happen to her. I have never been in love before but could this be it?" Matthew smiled as he rolled these thoughts over in his head. Just as he was about to be seated again at his desk, Theodora walked in. He looked at his watch to see that it was 4:00 PM. Where had the day gone?

"Good afternoon, Theodora," Matthew said. "Do you have any news for me?"

Theodora went over the day with him, all that had transpired at the press conference and the reports that had come in. She sat across from Matthew and looked at him as he bit down on the end of his pipe. Her eyes were warm and the President looked deeply into them.

Soon it was time to leave for the day so Theodora and Matthew said their goodbyes. When Theodora got back to her apartment she lay down on her bed still in her work outfit. She smiled as she thought about Matthew. She found herself thinking about him more and more these past few weeks. His face hardly left her mind and she thought he was the most handsome man she had ever met.

"Could this be love?" she thought to herself. "No it couldn't be." She paused and then thought, "But then maybe it is." She argued with herself as her mind went back and forth but she still remained in denial. She didn't want to admit to herself or anyone else that she was in love with the President, especially since she wasn't sure about his feelings for her.

After Theodora came down from the clouds, she started feeling rather distraught. How was this going to work out with God's plan? But maybe this was how God was going to work through it all. Suppose Matthew didn't care a thing about her? She was feeling confused and afraid. The President was still very much a part of the NWO and she dared not forget that. She decided it was best to try to put these feelings behind her. She needed to concentrate on the fact that Matthew was the President with whom she was working and nothing more.

Theodora undressed, took a shower and, after drying off and applying some fragrant body powder, slipped on a nightgown. As soon as her nightly routine was finished, she hopped into bed and opened her iPhone to discover there was a message on it. It was from Johnny saying that all was well but everybody missed her and hoped she could soon come home. She held the phone close to her bosom and prayed for everybody and their safety. After her nightly Bible reading, she slid under the covers and snapped off the light on her night stand. It wasn't long when she was dreaming sweet dreams about President Warner. In the morning she scolded herself for dreaming such things.

Chapter Thirty

A New Law

Theodora had left the office for the day when Bora stormed into the room.

"Matthew," she bellowed. "Take a look at this," and handed him the morning paper to read.

"It says that there is unrest in some of the large cities," he responded.

"Yes," Bora said, "and you know who the instigators are, don't you?"

"Who?" Matthew laid his pipe down and waited for the answer.

"It's those rabble rousers who call themselves Christians," Bora grunted. She seethed inside just thinking about the Christians. She hated them with a passion and always had. An evil grin crossed her face as she thought to herself, "Now I have the excuse to carry out my plan, one I have always dreamed of." She rubbed her hands together in delight.

"You can't blame the Christians. You don't know who is stirring up trouble. It could be anyone," Matthew remarked.

"Oh, you are always protecting the Christians," Bora shouted. "If I didn't know any better I would think you were one."

"You know better than to accuse me of that," Matthew retorted.

"Well we shall see about all this," Bora snapped as she headed on out the door.

"Now what could she possibly be up to now?" Matthew thought, shaking his head.

4:00 PM quickly rolled around and like clockwork Theodora walked in with a concerned expression on her face. "It seems like the riots are getting worse in New York and Chicago and they are spreading across the country. Some people are blaming the Christians for what is going on."

"Well, I'm not," Matthew assured. He knew Theodora had a certain tolerance of the Christians even though he didn't know why.

In the middle of Theodora's report for the day, Bora burst in.

"I've got the document ready," she announced.

"What is that?" Matthew asked.

"Here, read it," Bora demanded, fire in her voice.

After Matthew finished reading it, he put it down with a stern look. "You don't expect me to sign this, do you?"

"I do," Bora said, jutting her chin at Matthew.

"It says that all the Christians everywhere are to be killed. If approved by the NWO people everywhere will be instructed to kill their neighbor, their countryman, their families, everyone who claims to be a Christian or refuses to comply with the NWO. I can't sign this. I WON'T sign it." Matthew stood glaring at Bora with a belligerent demeanor, hands on hips.

"You can and you will," Bora demanded. "If you don't I have enough evidence against you to get you thrown out of office and executed."

Matthew scratched his chin. She was right. She did have the evidence. He had shown favor towards Theodora. For instance, he had given her unmerited time away from her duties along with extra days of unearned leave. This was a clear violation of the NWO code of ethics, a violation punishable by death. Matthew scratched his chin as he tried to recall giving special privileges to anyone else who had ever worked for him. He wasn't able to so Bora had him in a corner. Reluctantly he

153

signed the document which would go to the NWO headquarters in Brussels.

All the while Theodora was seated and listening with shock to all that was being said. Bora didn't try to hide any of it from her. In fact she wanted her to share it at the next press briefing in the morning. Bora gloated as she thought about it. She knew Theodora was sympathetic toward the Christians and she highly suspected her of even being one even though she couldn't prove it yet. She would just bide her time for now until she was presented with enough evidence to convict her. Her thoughts were filled with evil glee at the prospects of Theodora being strapped down on a table to be put to death. She had hated her from the beginning.

Watching the President pander to Theodora's every whim made Bora ill. She always had a close working relationship with Matthew over the years. To see his attention being drawn away from her towards another made her extremely jealous.

Bora contrived in her head a scheme to get even. "Just you wait, Theodora," she thought to herself. "I will have my revenge."

After signing the document, Matthew said, "Bora I am going by a postal station so I can take care of this today."

"Just see that you do, Matthew," Bora sternly warned.

Bora left and Theodora was sitting in a chair with her head down and her hands covering her face. She was weeping bitterly.

"Theodora, what's wrong?" Matthew asked tenderly.

"Oh, it's nothing," the girl replied, a touch of anger in her voice.

"Are you upset with me, Theodora? If I have done something to hurt you, please tell me what it is," Matthew begged. "I would never want you to feel disappointed in me."

"I guess I'm just tired," Theodora answered after a pause. "I'm not feeling very well either. I think I just need a leave of absence. After everything that has been happening I just need to go home to rest and be with my friends there."

Matthew took Theodora by the hand and sat by her. "You take all the time you need, my dear. I know you are disappointed with me for signing that document. But don't you understand? To not sign it would have meant a certain death sentence for me."

Theodora nodded weakly and then stood up. "Can I go now, sir?" she said coldly.

"Yes, you may leave. I hope you return soon," Matthew responded dully as she left the room. "She probably won't be back, not ever. I have lost her for good." He sat back down at his desk, staring glumly at the ceiling.

Theodora opened the door to her apartment and stepped into the room. As soon as she shook off her heels, she laid face-down on her bed for a good cry. When there were no more tears, she reached for her iPhone and sent an email to Johnny. "I'm coming home," she wrote and pushed the "send" button.

Back in Chota when Johnny received the brief email, he immediately knew something was wrong. He made a quick trip over to the White residence and knocked on the door. When it opened there stood Wilbur. By the look on Johnny's face, he knew something had happened to Theodora. "Come on in, Johnny," Wilbur said, an expression of concern in his voice as he motioned for him to sit down at the table.

Edna was right there with a cup of coffee for Johnny. "Can you tell us what happened?" she asked him.

"No! I just got a message that she is coming home. There was nothing else, nothing about how she was doing, no 'how is everybody,' no nothing," Johnny exclaimed. Worry creased his brow.

The room was silent for several moments and then Edna spoke up, "Oh what are we going to tell Theodora when she gets home? We never gave her the sad news about Adeline."

"Yes I know," Johnny said. "And it's a bad time to tell her now if she is having problems."

"Yes but she must be told," Wilbur sighed.

A month ago, Adeline had contracted pneumonia. The tribal doctor had used the best medicinal herbs that were available but she was old and her resistance was low. Adeline had just turned 86 years old and her heart had weakened with age. She had fought a good fight to defeat the disease but lost the battle in the end. They had buried her in the cemetery at the western edge of the village only two weeks ago. Edna still broke down in tears whenever she thought about Adeline.

Chapter Thirty-one

Home Again

Ralph Winters drove Theodora back to the little airport near Spruce Nob. He had a jeep similar to the one Clifford owned but this one was a tan color. It also had special security built into it as did all the vehicles the underground agents drove.

Johnny had been informed of the time and place the plane would be landing so he would be there ready to take Theodora back with him to Chota.

As planned, Johnny was there waiting when Theodora's plane landed. When she saw him, she ran up to him and embraced him, tears of joy running down her face. Johnny laughed and hugged her back. "I almost said, 'Let me take your suitcase' but I remember now that you left with none and of course you would return the same way."

"I do have clothes but I left them in my apartment in Washington DC. I didn't think I would need fancy duds here," Theodora laughed.

Theodora and Johnny chatted all the way back to Chota. She told him about her nightmare and her close call with the assailant, how she had been shot and nearly died.

"You must be careful there in Washington," Johnny remarked. "I told you before you left here that you would be stepping into a new world where danger lurks around every corner."

When they reached Chota, Theodora literally ran to her lodge where she hugged and kissed everybody. Then she noticed sad looks on their faces.

"What is it?" Theodora asked with alarm. She noticed her grandmother wasn't among them. "Is it Grandma? Tell me, is she ill? What happened?" Panic rose in her voice.

"Come and sit down, honey," Aunt Edna said, her voice cracking. She gently led Theodora to a chair next to the table.

"I'm afraid I have some sad news, dear," Edna continued. "Your grandma can no longer be with us."

"What? Why?" Theodora said with an expression of consternation crossing her face.

"She is in Heaven now," Edna said, a hand on Theodora's shoulder. Immediately the girl broke down in a river of tears. She cried for several minutes before she remembered what she had come home for.

"I...I've got to warn you," Theodora began.

"About what?" Edna asked.

"The President signed a document to send to the NWO and if they put it into affect no Christian will be safe anywhere anymore," Theodora went on.

Wilbur had been standing there and heard everything the girl had said. "What do you mean, Theodora?" he asked.

"This document states that every Christian is to be killed and citizens are commanded to carry this out. They are to kill their neighbors, family members, anyone who they suspect of being a Christian. The NWO blames the Christians for all the strife and unrest in the big cities. None of us is safe. Uncle Wilbur, you must take Aunt Edna and hide out in Painted Cavern.

"Calm down, Theodora," Wilbur soothed. "God has everything under His control. Don't you see this may be part of His plan?"

Theodora looked at her uncle in astonishment. "What? That's crazy! How could the destruction of His church be part of God's plan?"

"Don't you see, child?" Wilbur continued. "God has planted you in a strategic place for such a time as this."

"Such a time," Theodora repeated. "I remember Clifford telling me the same thing. Is God trying to tell me something?"

"Now we need to call the community together and declare a fast. After three days of fasting and praying, you are to return to Washington," Uncle Wilbur declared.

"B-But," Theodora protested. "I will be walking into a certain death trap."

"Not if God is with you," Wilbur promised.

Theodora was afraid and had many doubts. "I want to see Grandma's grave," she said.

"Of course," Wilbur responded. "Johnny and I will take you there.

They went to the cemetery which was well taken care of. The ground was well mown and lush green. Flowers were on all the graves. When Theodora saw where her grandmother was buried she saw a large bouquet of yellow daffodils lying at her headstone.

"Daffodils were her favorite flower," Theodora sobbed, dabbing at her eyes with a handkerchief. "Can I be alone with Grandma now?"

"Of course, dear," Uncle Wilbur said. "Take your time. We will wait for you back home."

Theodora looked at Adeline's resting place and began to talk to her as though she were standing before her. "Grandma," she began. "I don't know what to do. I wish you were here now. You always had an answer for me when I was afraid, and I'm afraid right now. I'm afraid to go back to Washington. I'm afraid of what might happen to me. Yet I'm afraid not to go. If it is God's will that I go, I don't want to disobey Him. Oh, Grandma, I need to know what to do." Theodora wept silently, wishing

159

Adeline was there to wrap her arms around her and comfort her as she did so often when she was a little girl.

For three solid days Pastor Soaring Eagle led his congregation in prayer. No one worked or played during this time. Their appeals and cries were lifted up towards Heaven as they pleaded for mercy, for their very lives. Even now the NEWOPS had discovered some of the hidden villages and were dragging leaders to places of execution. They caught some running for safety towards hidden caves. Some were shot on the spot while others were hauled away for interrogation followed by the cruelest form of execution.

Theodora had told Johnny about the brutal beatings back in Washington with victim's teeth knocked out and bones broken. Then they would be horribly executed by lethal injection with no anesthesia. Johnny shuddered when he heard all this. He couldn't imagine such inhumane treatment that was taking place everywhere outside the tribal villages.

When the three days of fasting and prayer were finished, Johnny came to visit Wilbur and Theodora a day later.

"I've been speaking with the pastor and all the elders and this is what God has been revealing to us," Johnny said. "Theodora is to return to Washington. It is time for her to reveal who she is to the President."

Blood drained from Theodora's face when she heard this. "He's got to be kidding," she thought. Then after thinking about it for a few minutes, she realized the tribal leaders had heard from God. They were practically always on the mark when they received a message from Him. She knew she had to respond to what she just heard. "If God said it, then I must obey." She held her head high. "I believe He can save me just like He saved Daniel when he was thrown into the lion's den. But if He doesn't spare me, I will not have died in vain."

Uncle Wilbur beamed with pride as he looked at his niece. Then he shared how God had revealed the same thing to him during the time of prayer. This confirmed the message Johnny brought to them.

"Theodora," Uncle Wilbur said. "There is something I want to give you before you leave."

"What is that, Uncle Wilbur?" Theodora asked.

"It's an old history book, one your grandmother brought all the way from Topeka. She wanted you to have it," Wilbur said. He went into his bedroom, dug through a dresser drawer and brought the book out to give to Theodora.

With tears, Theodora hugged and thanked her uncle. She would cherish it always and all the more since it was a gift from her beloved grandmother. Tears running down her cheeks, Theodora opened the book with its yellowed pages. As she thumbed through it, she recognized it as being very similar to one she had seen in the treasure cave so many years ago.

That night she would look at the pictures with the plan that she would thoroughly read it once she returned to Washington.

The next day, Theodora got ready to return to the little airport where the jet would be waiting to take her back to the city. Like before she would take nothing with her but the clothes on her back. The President had already been informed of her return. He had emailed a message stating that he was very pleased that she was coming back to work for him again.

Chapter Thirty-two

Collaboration with the Enemy

As Theodora was preparing for her return trip to Washington, something very sinister was taking place.

Bora paid a visit to the assassin who was being held in a cell underneath the White House. On her way she went down some stairs that were hidden behind a locked door. They led to two rooms situated underneath the basement. One of them contained a holding cell for prisoners. Right now it held Judd Parker, the man who had attempted to assassinate the President. The other one was quite empty and not being used for anything.

Bora took a key to the cell and let herself in. Judd was asleep on a cot next to a grey wall. There were no windows in the room, only bars at the door.

"Get up," Bora demanded, shaking Judd awake.

"WH-What do you want?" Judd mumbled sleepily. He rubbed his eyes in order to clearly see who was disturbing him. "Bora," he exclaimed and then he smiled. "How are you, my friend?"

"This is no time for formalities," Bora answered. "I have another job for you to do and this time you had better not fail."

"It wasn't my fault that I got caught," Judd protested. "This place is all eyes. You can't make a move around here without being seen."

"No more excuses," Bora bellowed. "Here is what I want you to do." She proceeded to tell him her scheme.

"Does that mean you are letting me out?" Judd asked.

"Yes but you better do the job right this time or you will find yourself in that other room being injected with poison," Bora warned. "And like all the others you won't be given the mercy of an anesthetic first."

"If I succeed this time, what is in it for me?" Judd demanded.

"When I am President, MAYBE I will ask the NWO chief if I can make you my VP. But that isn't a promise," Bora frowned.

"Well what if I don't want to go through with it," Judd scoffed.

"Then you will have chosen lethal injection," Bora scowled.

"I can see you leave me with no choice. When do you want the job done?" Judd growled.

"Within the week," Bora answered. "I will be back with the key to release you when everything is ready."

Bora left the cell and returned to the Oval Office where she had an appointment with President Warner. He was waiting for her with a smile on his face.

"What are you grinning at?" Bora grumbled.

"Theodora is returning today. Isn't that great," Matthew answered.

"Yeah, just great," Bora muttered begrudgingly. "Well let's forget about her and get down to business."

That afternoon, Ralph Winters met Theodora at the airport in Spruce Nob to take her back to Washington DC. On the way Theodora shared the plan with Ralph.

"This is amazing," Ralph commented. "We have been praying for you while you were gone and God shared this very same plan with us. Something great is going to come out of all this."

Theodora beamed and any fear she had carried with her vanished. She knew now that God would protect her. She didn't know how but she knew He would.

When she arrived at her apartment, Theodora looked in her closet to see her clothes hanging the same way she had left them. Nothing had been disturbed and nobody had been there during the time she had been away. Theodora breathed a sigh of relief knowing that she had not yet been discovered.

The next morning Theodora greeted the President with a big smile. He flashed a smile back showing his straight white teeth. He put his pipe in his mouth and lit it. "How have you been?" he said.

"Oh it was a most relaxing time for me," Theodora answered. "I enjoyed being with my friends again. We had such a good time." It wasn't exactly a lie. She had relaxed part of the time and she certainly was among friends.

"I am so happy to hear that," Matthew grinned. "Oh, how good it is to have you back! You don't know how much I missed you."

Bora was seated in one of the stuffed chairs towards the back of the room. "Oh how good it is! How good it is!" she repeated sarcastically to herself. "I will be rid of that little trouble maker if I have anything to do with it." Her hatred of Theodora grew testier by the day but she was careful not to show how she felt to Matthew.

Chapter Thirty-three

Bora's Little Surprise

As the days went by, Bora was suspiciously kind to
Theodora. One day she even surprised her with a bottle of
perfume.

"Why, thank you, Bora! That happens to be my favorite.
How did you know?" Theodora smiled and took the bottle.

"Matthew told me," Bora answered. "I knew your
birthday was coming up so I thought I would give you an early
present."

"How thoughtful of you, Bora," Theodora exclaimed as she
was putting the perfume into her purse. "I will always remember
you for that."

As the days went by, Theodora marveled at the change in
Bora. "God must be working on her," she thought. "I shouldn't
be surprised though. God is capable of changing the most
hardened hearts."

A week went by and Theodora was getting ready to
celebrate her 22nd birthday the next day. "May I use the State
White House dining room to celebrate?" she asked Matthew.
"My birthday is tomorrow and I want to invite everyone to my
party, including you and Bora."

"Certainly," Matthew replied. "You can use the kitchen
staff to prepare a meal too, anything that you would like." The
President was pleased, yet surprised with the way Bora and
Theodora had been getting along lately. He hadn't experienced
such peace since Theodora had first come to Washington.

The next day, Theodora was getting the dining room ready
for the sumptuous feast that was about to be served. The guests
were already entering the great dining room and soon friendly

chatter filled the room. Soft dinner music flowed through the amplifiers that were situated on the wall on either side of the fireplace. This lent a pleasant atmosphere to the room and everything couldn't have been any finer.

Soon the guests were seated and a feast of quail, asparagus, and sweet potatoes baked in a sweet maple glaze were brought out. This had been preceded by steaming bowls of lobster bisque followed by Caesar salad. After everyone had enjoyed the main meal, the kitchen maids brought out a luscious dessert of flambéed vanilla-poached pears with apricot sauce.

When everybody finished their meal, they generously complimented Theodora and the chefs. Then the birthday presents were brought out for her to open.

"Thank you, everybody, for coming," Theodora exclaimed as everyone was getting ready to leave. "I don't remember ever having such a nice birthday party. I love parties and I will make sure that you are all invited to the next one."

Bora gently took Theodora by the arm and said, "Don't leave yet, my dear. I have another surprise for you. Please come with me."

Theodora gladly followed wondering what the surprise could be. She trailed after Bora to the basement where Bora unlocked the door to the stairs leading to the rooms below. Everything had a musty smell and Theodora started to feel uneasy. Why was Bora taking her down there? But she had been so nice to her. How could anything be wrong? Yet it did seem a little strange for Bora to be taking her into a place like this.

Theodora cast all suspicion aside and continued to follow Bora who unlocked the door leading into the little empty room beside the prison cell. But it wasn't empty.

Without warning Bora shoved Theodora in and then slammed and locked the door behind her. To the girl's utter horror, there stood the three NEWOPS she had seen in her nightmare - Dutch, Thomas and Timothy. They all waited there, a dark threatening look on their faces.

Theodora looked all around the room. It was exactly like the one she had seen in her dream, stark white walls and a table with straps on it.

Theodora started to scream as the men inched towards her, reaching out to grab her. After a brief moment of panic, she remembered her training. She decided to go after the big one first. In a blur of whirling kicks and karate jabs, she knocked Dutch to the floor. Suddenly Timothy turned on the other one. After a brief battle he was finally able to overpower his opponent with a blow to the head.

Afterward both Theodora and Timothy looked down at their combatants who were now lying on the floor. Both Dutch and Thomas were dead from fatal blows to the head.

Theodora looked up at Timothy with an expression of utter surprise.

"Why did you save me?" Theodora asked.

"It's a long story but right now we have to get rid of these bodies before anyone discovers them," Timothy said. They discovered a small cubby hole hidden in a closet of the room and stuffed the bodies into it. "Nobody will ever find them here. Now I need to find a place for you to hide out in until it is safe," Timothy continued. He took her by the hand and led her through a tunnel leading from the room. This finally met another room that nobody ever used and few had even seen.

The room was dark and painted grey with no carpeting or rugs on the floor. There was no furniture in the room, only a picture of President Abraham Lincoln that hung on a wall.

"How curious!" Theodora thought as she looked at the picture. "I didn't think any pictures of this sort were left by the NWO. They must not have discovered this one yet."

To Timothy's knowledge only the President knew about this place. Being the White House janitor he had access to every nook and cranny of the White House. One day when he was in the basement cleaning, he discovered this little hide-away.

By some fluke, Timothy found the President's secret diary in that room. This had been passed down from President to President and it contained a detailed map of the White House. It included all the secret tunnels and passageways which nobody was supposed to know about other than the President himself. The diary was kept locked up in a vault with a combination that only the President was privy to. This safe was hidden behind a wall which was covered by the picture of President Lincoln.

One day the President grew careless. In a hurry to get to a meeting, he forgot to lock the safe. That night, when Timothy was exploring the secret room some more, he saw the open vault. The picture which had been used to cover it now lay against the wall on the floor where the President had left it.

Timothy found the diary still inside the safe. Since it was late and nobody was around, he took it and studied it. Afterward, using a flashlight, he followed the map to the various secret rooms and passageways. After that he carefully put the diary back in the vault exactly the way he had found it so as not to pique the President's suspicions. This discovery hadn't been by coincidence. It was all a part of God's plan.

Timothy had never looked at the diary again since that night. From then on, he had to rely on his memory to find the secret room where Theodora was now hiding.

As soon as Timothy had Theodora safely situated, he warned her, "Do not venture from this place until I come for you.

It could be a while before it is safe for you to leave. I will be right back with some water and food for you." Timothy left and was back within an hour with some bottles of water and food rations which had been stowed away to be used in case of emergencies. He also carried a blanket with him but no pillow.

"I'm afraid," Theodora admitted.

"You will be fine. I won't let anything happen to you," Timothy assured her before he left again.

The room was dark except for a small light bulb that wasn't much brighter than a night light. It cast eerie shadows against the drab walls and ceiling. Theodora sighed as she tried to make herself comfortable on the hard surface of the floor. She searched around for something to lay her head on but found nothing. She was thankful for the blanket though because the room was unheated, damp and cold. The blanket was heavy and made of wool which provided the adequate warmth she needed.

During her wait, Theodora searched around and found a small room adjacent to the one she was in. The single door leading into it wasn't locked. When Theodora opened it up she saw an old slop bucket but nothing else. There was no mirror or wash basin or any place to shower. Theodora was happy for the makeshift toilet though as that was the most necessary item at the time.

Theodora fiddled with her blanket as she thought about the little room she was hiding in. This room must have been used by someone at one time who had to stow away here as she now did. "Maybe it was during the Civil War," she imagined. "Maybe it was used by a slave who was trying to escape from the South."

Theodora lost all sense of time but she knew several days, perhaps even a week had passed. Loneliness plagued her but she was glad she had Jesus to talk to. He seemed to fill the empty hours with his presence and she talked to Him as she would her grandmother if she was there. The Holy Spirit brought comforting scripture to her mind along with many promises. Theodora recited Psalm 23, knowing that the Lord was truly her Shepherd and wouldn't allow anything to happen to her outside of His will. She might die physically but her soul and spirit were safe with Him.

Chapter Thirty-four

Murder Plot

A week had gone by and Theodora hadn't shown up for work.

"Do you know what has happened to Theodora?" Matthew asked Bora.

"No, I'm sorry," Bora answered. "I haven't heard from her. I thought you knew where she was."

"She sent me a message telling me she was sick but that was several days ago and I haven't heard a word from her since," Matthew remarked. "It isn't like Theodora to not check in with me every day, sick or not."

Bora had sent the email to Matthew making it look like it had come from Theodora. She knew every trick in the book including how to hack into somebody else's computer. She was very clever in her evil schemes and her soul was now totally demon possessed.

Bora had been in contact with NWO headquarters on a daily basis. She snooped around the Oval Office and even looked through the President's desk drawers.

One day as Bora was prying through the papers in his desk, she came across a manila envelope. She opened it to find the document the President had supposedly mailed to the NWO a few months back. As soon as she discovered it, she vowed to do away with Matthew. That was when she paid her visit to the would-be assassin, Judd, to plan the President's murder.

It was evening around 7:00 PM and President Warner was still in his office going through some reports. He had decided to use a substitute for Press Secretary until Theodora was back on her feet.

Outside the sun was going down. Matthew looked up from his work to admire the glorious sunset with all its pastel colors of pink, purple, orange and yellow.

As Matthew resumed the task of poring through his papers, Bora burst into the room.

"Here he is," she shouted, pointing at the President. Judd ran into the Oval Office after her with a loaded pistol, cocked and ready to fire at the President. He was taking careful aim when a shot was heard behind him. Judd cried out, and then crumpled in agony as he fell to the floor. With a gun smoking in his hand, Timothy Everest stepped into the room.

With shock and dismay, Matthew looked at Bora. "Bora, why? How could you do this to me? Why would you want to kill me?"

"I had to," Bora barked. "You are a threat to our cause. You have turned on me and the NWO. You are a traitor and deserve to die. I should be President, not you."

Two security guards rushed into the room.

"Arrest her," Matthew said pointing to Bora. As the guards grabbed her, Matthew spoke a few more words to his Vice-President. "You will be executed by lethal injection but I won't leave you in agony as you have left your victims. I will make sure you are anesthetized first."

Bora turned to Matthew and said in a sadistic tone, "Before I go, I will tell you where your Theodora is. She is dead. She has been executed with that lethal chemical and I made sure they didn't use any anesthesia on her. I heard her scream as she was dying." Although Bora thought the girl was dead, she deliberately lied about hearing her scream in order to leave Matthew in mental torment. She wanted her final revenge against Matthew before she died. As she was being hauled away down the hall, her evil laughter could be heard all the way.

Matthew let out a groan as he bent over his desk and wept loudly, his body shaking. Looking at him with compassion, Timothy came over and laid a hand on his shoulder.

"She isn't dead," Timothy said.

Matthew looked up. "What did you say?"

"She isn't dead," Timothy repeated. "She is safe. I hid her away." He proceeded to tell Matthew about the escape and all that had happened afterward.

Matthew could scarcely believe the good news. "Where is she?"

"I will get her and bring her to you." Timothy turned to leave but Matthew extended a hand towards him.

"I want to thank you, son. What is your name?" Matthew inquired. Timothy told him and Matthew continued, "You will be greatly rewarded for your heroism. Now go and get Theodora for me."

Chapter Thirty-five

The Plan Unfolding

Theodora stood before Matthew silently as she prayed to herself for the strength to say what she had to. She stood staring at him for a few moments and Matthew looked straight into her eyes. There was softness there but would it still be there after he learned the truth?

Finally Theodora opened her mouth. "Please have mercy on me and my family."

"Why of course! Why wouldn't I?" Matthew was perplexed that she would say such a thing.

"I don't quite know how to tell you this," Theodora continued. "I came here under false pretenses. I'm not who you think I am."

"Oh?" Matthew was getting really confused now. "What are you trying to tell me, Theodora?"

"I'm a Christian, one of those rebels Bora talks about. But, sir, this isn't what we are at all. Our God sent His Son, Jesus, to bring peace to the earth and we are His followers. We don't want to make trouble for anyone. We only want to share the good news about Jesus. He has come to bring salvation, healing and hope to those who will receive Him." Matthew looked at her expressionless. Theodora didn't know how to read him.

"Please, sir, don't have me executed. I beg you. Please have mercy on me," Theodora cried. "I know we have been blamed for all the riots and trouble in the big cities. But it isn't our doing. It is the NEWOPS who are doing this. They dress in plain clothes and pretend to be one of us. Then they wreak havoc so we Christians will be killed for something we didn't do. Don't you understand; the NWO has used this to plot against us. This is their way of getting rid of us."

Matthew looked stunned and then left the room abruptly.

Theodora was sure that the President would return with guards to arrest her. The plan didn't work. She was doomed to be executed. Her nightmare was about to become reality and this time she would be helpless to escape. She stood there in the middle of the Oval Office and wept bitterly.

After several minutes, Matthew returned and looked at Theodora. He smiled and placed a reassuring hand on her shoulder. "My dear, I wouldn't harm a hair on your head." Theodora couldn't believe her ears.

"I thought it all over while I was out of the office," Matthew continued. "At first I thought about having you executed because, by not doing so, I would become an enemy of the State. But I just couldn't bring myself to do that."

"Oh, Matthew, what made you change your mind?" Theodora looked at him with compassion in her eyes.

"I can't bear the thoughts of losing you, Theodora. Don't you see? I'm in love with you." He put his arms around her and then gently kissed her.

"Oh Matthew!" Theodora cradled her head on his chest and placed her arms around his broad shoulders. "What are we going to do? We are going to both be killed by the NEWOPs."

"I don't know, my dear. I will have to think on it for a while. They won't come after us for a while yet. Perhaps I can think of something by then." Matthew's voice trailed off as he reached for his pipe. He always seemed to smoke a pipe when he was reflecting on something.

Theodora couldn't bear to think of the prospects of being executed any longer so she changed the subject to a more pleasant one. "I have a book for you to read. I brought it with me when I came into the office a couple of weeks ago. I think I left it over there somewhere." Theodora went over to a small desk and opened the middle drawer. "Here it is. I want you to read it. It will explain a lot to you about how this country was started and who the great leaders of the past were." She handed the book to Matthew.

"American History," Matthew read aloud from the cover. "I always did want to know our history. History was my favorite subject in school but I always wondered if I was getting the truth back then when I was growing up."

"This is the truth, Matthew. The history taught in this book is authentic. It was printed before the books were altered to fit the schemes of the secular humanists and atheists." Theodora opened the book for him to see pictures of the Mayflower bringing pilgrims to Plymouth Rock. They were celebrating their first Thanksgiving and missionaries were carrying the gospel to the Indians. Matthew was intrigued by how the first settlers risked their lives to come to America so they could be free. In the back of the book was a copy of the Constitution and Declaration of Independence.

"Wow!" Matthew exclaimed. "I had no idea. May I take this and read it tonight? I want to get together with you tomorrow to discuss this with you some more. I will probably have a lot of questions too. By the way, where did you get this book?"

"It's a gift from my grandmother," Theodora said. "You may take the book but please be very careful with it. I wouldn't want anything to happen to it. I treasure it as if it were made of gold because it belonged to my grandmother and I loved her so."

"My dear, I will be sure and return it to you in the same condition as it is now," the President assured with a big smile.

Theodora was radiant. God had given her favor. He had kept His promise to her that He would protect her. His plan was really becoming clear to her now.

After Theodora retired for the night, she could hardly wait until morning to get together with Matthew again.

In the White House apartments, Matthew was devouring the history book. He wasn't able to put it down until he had finished it around 3:00 in the morning. He could hardly grasp what he had read but deep down inside he knew it was true. Theodora wouldn't give him anything that wasn't. She was the most truthful, sincere person he had ever met.

When Theodora arrived at the White House at 8:00 sharp the next morning, she wondered how she would make a report about this to the press. She shared her dilemma with Matthew.

"Not to worry, Theodora," he assured. "It's all under control. I put out a statement before you came this morning. There will be no more press conferences or briefings for the rest of the week. I plan to spend all my time here with you."

"Oh good! I want to talk with you too. There is so much I want to tell you." Theodora sat comfortably in her favorite stuffed chair near the President's desk.

All that day, they discussed the founding fathers, the Constitution and Declaration of Independence. Matthew couldn't get over the fact that people had the freedom to speak what they wanted without getting arrested. He had a lot of questions about Christians and church. What did they do and what did they believe? Why were they baptized and why did they give their allegiance to a man who died millennia ago?

Theodora tried her best to explain but she knew he couldn't understand unless the Holy Spirit revealed it to him. In the mean time she told him about the American flag and the way it used to look before it had been replaced by the NWO banner. She pointed out a picture of one in the history book.

Matthew's face lit up then. "I think I have one stowed away in one of my desk drawers, one I hardly ever use. I had put it there years ago and forgotten all about it since then." He got up and fumbled through all the drawers. When he found the flag he pulled it out of the drawer and held it up.

"Where did you ever get that?" Theodora asked her eyes wide with surprise.

"It was a souvenir I picked up a long time ago. I can't remember just where though," Matthew remarked. Then he took a good look at the flag.

"Wow!" he exclaimed as he held it up. "It is so beautiful, even proud looking. The founding fathers must have had some kind of invisible hand guiding them when they created this."

"That was the hand of God," Theodora explained. "This country was planned and inspired by God as He directed our founding fathers in the development of it. Our Constitution had to be divinely inspired because it lasted longer than any other in the world for all time. It wasn't until people turned their backs on God that the Constitution was abrogated. After that the country's foundation crumbled and the nation fell into enemy hands."

"You think the NWO is the enemy then?" Matthew asked.

"Yes! Look at the way the NEWOPS treat people, brutally torturing them and then killing them. Would a loving God do that? The NWO isn't God's creation. It has been set up by Satan himself."

Things began to come into focus more clearly for Matthew. He had watched Theodora for nearly a year now since she first came to work for him. She had displayed nothing but peace and love and forgiveness towards the people who worked for a cruel, unjust system. When she told him about Jesus and how much He loved him it was starting to sink in.

About a week later, after several days of discussion, the Holy Spirit brought back to memory something that had happened in Matthew's childhood. "Theodora, I have begun to remember something from my past, something I had forgotten," Matthew began.

"What is that?" Theodora looked at him inquisitively.

"I remember my grandmother holding me on her lap when I was about four-years-old," Matthew continued. "She used to tell me Bible stories. I had forgotten that. For some reason she was raising me. I must have had no parents. I didn't remember them any way."

He paused and reflected on his past, puffing on his pipe. Then he shared some more. "I liked the way it felt when my grandmother prayed with me. I think I remember a little prayer she taught me."

Matthew put his pipe down and looked seriously at Theodora. "Theodora, I want to know this God of yours. I want to know Him like you do. Will you pray with me?"

"Yes, Matthew! Take my hands and kneel down here with me," she said, smiling. They knelt down on the rug in the Oval Office and soon it became a room of prayer. The entire room emanated a glow that seemed to come from nowhere and yet it came from everywhere. When they got up off their knees, Matthew was a new person, saved and washed clean by the blood of Jesus. His countenance literally shone and he thought he could hear the angels sing.

"Matthew, what are we going to do?" Theodora's expression turned to one of concern.

"God will show us. I am going to ask Him. Give me a week to pray about this. I am sure God will guide me," Matthew assured. "In one week from today I will have the answer for you."

Theodora was amazed at the spiritual insight Matthew had already. But she knew He now was filled with the Holy Spirit. The President was allowing the Lord to control his thoughts now. This was where he was getting his wisdom.

That week seemed to drag on forever for Theodora. What was God going to show Matthew? What final plan did God have?

Chapter Thirty-six

The Plan Fulfilled

Finally the day came for Theodora to return to the Oval Office. Matthew was there already waiting. His face was beaming and she knew He had met with God. She was filled with anticipation and excitement.

"Sit down, Theodora," Matthew began. "Several things have happened since we were together last. One night as I was praying, God spoke to me and told me to expect a call from a man, a Native American." Theodora perked up when he said that.

"Who?" she asked with excitement.

"When I got the call, the man on the other end of the line said his name was Johnny Fast Horse," Matthew answered. "Is that name familiar to you?"

"Why yes! He is the one who rescued me and my family and hid us away in his village." Theodora waited for him to continue.

"He gave me a message from God," Matthew said.

"Tell me...Tell me," Theodora pleaded. She was so excited she nearly leapt out of her chair.

"Here it is and I have already carried out part of the instructions given to me." Matthew smiled and looked out the window, then back at Theodora. "I was told that the Prime Minister of Israel is our friend and he can be trusted. Israel never became a part of the NWO. He also told me that there were two other regions along with ours that were ready to pull out of the World Government."

Theodora listened in astonishment as the President continued. "I have already talked to the Prime Minister of Israel and will soon be setting up a private meeting with the leaders of the other two regions. We will pool our resources. After some research I learned that there is a lot of oil under the earth in certain parts of the country that hadn't yet been tapped into. There are also oil wells that have been capped since the NWO took over. All fossil fuels were outlawed then and haven't been used since; these have only been available to those who are very wealthy or in powerful positions in the NWO. The NWO have used the rich to achieve their own ends. When they are through with them they will cast them aside like dirty rags."

"That explains why everybody is poor and travel is so limited" Theodora added. "The Cheyenne and other tribes have acclimated to it, though, by going back to their old ways. They have vehicles that are hidden away only to be used in cases of emergencies. Somehow they managed to stash away enough fuel to last until the nation could be returned to us. They have provided the underground agents with fuel also. There are tanks hidden underground in strategic places all over the country but they know they have to be very frugal lest they run out of the precious liquid gold."

"There is one more thing I need to do today," Matthew said. He stood up and grabbed the NWO flag, tearing it off its pole and trampling it on the ground. "Theodora, can you help me with this please?" He held up the American flag for her to take one part of and together they put it on the flag pole in place of the old banner from Hell.

"That looks so beautiful," Theodora commented.

"Yes, doesn't it!" Matthew agreed.

"Theodora, I want to ask you something before you leave," Matthew said, looking into her eyes and cradling her face in his hands.

"Yes," Theodora answered with anticipation.

"I need you to be by my side if we are going to get this country back to the way it used to be," Matthew said. "Will you marry me?"

Theodora's eyes lit up as she threw her arms about him. "Oh yes! I will! I certainly will."

The End

Books Written by Adrienne Hartman

"Living Stones" – A book of 52 testimonies

"These Stones Cry Out" – A second book of 52 testimonies

"Banner of Courage" – A novel

All of these books are available on Amazon.

31927541R00107

Made in the USA
San Bernardino, CA
23 March 2016